SINISTER SPIDERS
OF
SAGINAW

Look for more 'Michigan Chillers' from AudioCraft Publishing, Inc., including:

AudioCraft Publishing, Inc.
PO Box 281
Topinabee Island, MI 49791

#9: Sinister Spiders
of
Saginaw

Johnathan
Rand

An AudioCraft Publishing, Inc. book

Graphics layout/design consultant: Chuck Beard, Straits Area Printing

Book warehouse and storage facilities provided by Clarence and Dorienne's Storage, Car Rental & Shuttle Service, Topinabee Island, MI

ISBN 1-893699-15-3

Printed in USA

Second Printing, July 2001

Sinister Spiders
of
Saginaw

Visit the official 'Michigan Chillers' web site at:

www.michiganchillers.com

Featuring excerpts from upcoming stories, interviews, contests, official Michigan Chillers wearables, and *more!*

There were two things that happened that day that should have given me a clue as to what was about to come. The first thing happened when I was doing my homework.

It was five-thirty in the morning. I like getting up early to work on my homework. It's really quiet, and my older brother isn't awake to bug me. I was at the dining table, working on my math. Mom had just woke up, and she came into the kitchen.

"My goodness, Leah," she yawned as she

strode into the room. "How long have you been up?"

"Not long," I replied, putting my pencil down. "I just need to go over the answers on my homework."

Leah is my name. Leah Warner. I'm thirteen, and I live just outside of the Saginaw city limits. It's a pretty cool city, and there's a lot of history here. Saginaw began in 1816 as a fur-trading post. The name 'Saginaw', like a lot of Michigan cities, is actually a Native American name. 'O-Sag-A-Nong' means 'land of the Sauks'. That's where the word 'Saginaw' comes from.

But after what was about to happen, you might call Saginaw the 'land of the spiders.'

I *hate* spiders. I absolutely *hate* them. I mean, I know that they serve their purpose and everything, by eating bugs and stuff, but spiders are just so . . . *gross.* They're fine if they leave me alone, but if I see one in my house, he's history.

Like the one that was climbing on my leg that morning.

Mom had just left the kitchen, and I returned to my homework. I had my nose in a book, and was double-checking the answers on my math paper. We were going to have a quiz today. Ug.

I felt a light tickling on my ankle, and I looked down.

It was a spider! Not a big one, mind you — but that didn't matter. It was a *spider*, and it was crawling on *me*. I about jumped out of my skin!

"*Yaaaa!*" I shrieked, dropping my pencil and smacking my leg with the palm of my hand. The awful bugger crushed under my hard slap, and, as I wiped him away, the tiny creature balled up and fell to the floor, dead.

"Eewww," I moaned, staring down at the lifeless, crumpled-up spider on the floor.

Our dog, Grumpy, heard me scream, and he waddled into the room. Grumpy is a brown cocker spaniel. If you wake him up from a sleep, he lays on the ground and growls at you. Oh, he'd never bite you. He's just grumpy — and that's how he got his name. My older brother, Scott, found him as a puppy. We've had Grumpy for almost five years.

Grumpy walked over to me, sniffed the floor — *and ate the dead spider!*

"Eeeww!! Grumpy!" I scolded, wincing. "That's sick!" Grumpy wagged his tail, turned around, and bounded happily away.

Silly dog. I can't believe he would actually eat

a spider!

Of course, a lot of things were about to happen that I wouldn't believe. Things that I wouldn't have imagined in a million years.

Later that day, after school, I rode the bus home and sprinted to the front door of our house. We live on Hamilton Street, and our house is only a mile from my school. Sometimes I ride my bike. Scott almost always rides his bike, except in the winter, so he usually makes it home before I do. The bus ride can be kind of long.

I burst through the door, my backpack in hand—and froze in horror.

There, on the living room floor, was a spider! Not just a spider—but a tarantula!

2

A wave of terror shuddered through my body. The spider was huge, ugly, and *nasty*. It was the biggest spider I've ever seen! It was black and brown, and looked like it had fur all over its body. Two big, black eyes stared menacingly back at me. The spider was the most hideous, horrible creature I'd ever seen in my life.

Grumpy was there, his hackles raised and teeth bared. He was only a few feet away from the spider. He snarled and snapped, but he kept his distance from the enormous creature on the carpet.

My backpack fell to the floor, and my mouth opened wide. I tried to scream, but no sound would come out. My whole body shook.

Suddenly, the spider *moved!* One of his legs raised up slowly, and the spider inched toward me.

This was a nightmare! Worse . . . it was really happening! Oh, how I *wished* it was a nightmare. Then I could wake up!

But this wasn't any dream at all. There was a spider—a *huge* one—not five feet away from me!

Grumpy continued to snarl and bark, but he kept his distance. This was one spider he was *not* going to eat!

I stood there, unable to move, when I suddenly heard snickering coming from the hall. I saw a shadow move, then I heard more giggling.

Suddenly, Scott came into the living room wearing a mischievous grin. He walked right over to the spider . . . and picked it up!

"Like my pet?" he said, placing the spider in his palm.

Wait a minute, I thought. *There's something kind of strange about that spider . . . .*

Bravely, I took a step forward, my eyes focused

on the ugly, dark creature in Scott's hand.

"Check it out," he urged. "But be careful. He might bite you."

Closer . . . .

"You goofball!" I suddenly cried. "That's not a *real* spider!"

And it wasn't! Now that I had a closer look, I could see that the spider wasn't real, after all. It was fake! A very *good* fake, at that. But it really looked like an *actual* spider!

"Cool, huh?" he said, still wearing a cat-like grin. "I bought it at the gag-gift store. It was on sale." He flipped it over in his hand, pointing to an on/off switch on the spider's belly. He clicked the switch off. "See? It's battery-operated."

"Yeah, real cool," I snapped. I punched him in the shoulder so hard that he dropped the toy spider.

"Ouch!" he exclaimed. *"That hurt!"* He bent over to pick up the spider.

"You deserved it!" I said angrily, storming past him. My anger boiled, and I stomped across the living room and into my bedroom, slamming the door behind me.

Brothers, I thought, shaking my head. *They should be illegal. Brothers should be against the law.*

But there was one thing that made me happy. Today was Thursday . . . and Scott would be leaving for band camp tomorrow morning. He'd be gone for two whole days! Hurray! Not only that, it was a 'teacher in-service' day, which meant we wouldn't have any school Friday! I couldn't wait. Two whole days of peace and quiet. No Scott, no stupid pranks. Just me and Mom and Dad and Grumpy.

Peace and quiet.

Of course, peace and quiet was the last thing that I would have. I certainly didn't know it then, but soon, I would encounter spiders—real spiders—that were a hundred times bigger than the fake tarantula Scott had scared me with!

3

Friday morning, I slept in. The house was quiet until Scott woke up. He began racing around the house, looking for this and that, trying to pack all of his clothes at the last minute. As for me, I was snuggled in bed doing simple math in my head. I was counting the seconds until Scott would leave for band camp.

After he left, I made some toast and a cup of hot chocolate. The warm liquid tasted sweet and good. Mmmmmmm . . . I was feeling better already. Scott had only been gone five minutes, and I was already more relaxed. No pranks, no stupid jokes for two whole days. No dorky brother hanging around the house, bugging me.

Just Mom, Dad, Grumpy and myself.

Cool! I was in such a good mood that morning that I went for a walk in the park, just by myself, enjoying the day, taking my time, breathing in the fresh spring air.

■■■

When I returned, Mom and Dad had already left for work, so I found the hidden key to let myself in. We have a house key that we keep under a rock next to the porch, but don't tell anyone.

I found the key, unlocked the door, let myself in—and right away, I knew something was wrong. I could just *feel* it. I was overcome by a strange uneasiness that seeped into the pores of my skin.

What was it?

I stopped in the doorway, looking around the living room. Everything *looked* normal. Nothing was out of place. The house was silent, which wouldn't be unusual.

But it was *too* silent.

What was it? What was wrong?

And suddenly, I knew.

Grumpy. He always greets me at the door. He greets *everyone* at the door. He's usually at the door two seconds after he hears it open.

But not today.

"Grumpy?" I called out loudly, stepping into the living room. Maybe he was sleeping soundly, and hadn't heard me come home. I expected him to come running . . . but he didn't. The house was strangely quiet.

"Grumpy?" I hollered again, raising my voice even louder.

No dog. This was really weird.

I walked into the kitchen and found a yellow sticky-note on the fridge. It read:

Leah

Your father and I will both be working late tonight . . . should be home around eight. Make yourself a sandwich for lunch. For dinner, there's some leftover lasagna in the refrigerator – just nuke it for a few minutes. Oh...I let Grumpy outside. Can you let him in when you get back from your walk? Call me at the office if you *need anything. Love ya lots!*

—Mom

So that was it. Grumpy was outside, in the backyard. I relaxed, and walked to the sliding glass door to let Grumpy in. Our back yard has a fence that goes all the way around it. Grumpy can run and play in our yard without wandering off.

But Grumpy was nowhere to be found! He wasn't in the backyard.

"Grumpy!" I shouted, my voice echoing out over the yard. "Come here, boy!"

Unseen birds chirped from trees, and I could hear the happy laughter of little kids in our neighbor's yard.

But no Grumpy. I looked around, and I suddenly realized what had happened.

Grumpy likes to dig holes. And today, he'd dug a hole right under the fence! Grumpy had ran away!

Shoot, I thought. Once in a while, Grumpy gets out of the yard and wanders the neighborhood. He usually doesn't go too far, but we have to go look for him.

Which is what I would have to do. I couldn't

bear the thought of Grumpy wandering into a road or a highway. I had to find him . . . *fast.*

But I wasn't going to search for him alone. I called up Angela Meyer and Conner Karpinski, two of my best friends. Both live only a few houses away. They rushed over to help me find Grumpy.

"Where did you see him last?" Conner asked, placing his hands on his hips and looking around the front yard. Conner is twelve, but he's taller than I am. Actually, he's the tallest kid in our grade. He's got really blonde hair, the color of ripe corn.

"Well, I haven't seen him since this morning," I replied. "When I got home from a walk, he was gone. He'd dug a hole under the fence and crawled under it."

"He can't be far," Angela offered hopefully. She sounded positive and optimistic. That's one of the things I like about Angela: she always looks on the bright side of things. I've known Angela since the second grade. Her family came to the United States from a small town in South Africa. She tells me fascinating stories about what it was like to live there when she was younger.

We decided that, to find Grumpy quickly, we'd have to split up. I would go north and search a few blocks over, while Conner would go across the street and search some of the alleys and back streets.

Angela said she would go down near the old drainage ditch where the forest is really thick. It's kind of a swampy area, with lots of trees and muck, and I've never hung around there much. Nobody does. There are a lot of weird stories about the drainage ditch . . . crazy, bizarre stories. I've always ignored the stories, because they were too weird to be true.

But I've stayed away, just in case.

I searched and searched for nearly an hour without any luck. Conner hadn't spotted Grumpy, either, and we finally met up again at our house. We waited for Angela.

And we waited.

But Angela never came back. She never returned, which wasn't like Angela at all.

So we decided to go look for her . . . at the old drainage ditch a few blocks away.

And what we were about to encounter was the scariest, freakiest thing that had ever happened to me in my entire life.

4

The drainage ditch isn't far from where we live. Conner and I walked down the sidewalk, completely unaware of the terrible circumstances that were about to befall us.

"Where does Grumpy like to go when he runs off?" Conner asked.

"All over the place," I answered, rolling my eyes. "Grumpy just likes cruising around and checking things out."

We kept our eyes peeled as we walked, looking

for signs of the dog. Once, I spotted a movement in a yard, but it was someone else's dog.

Soon, we came to the old drainage ditch — and right away, we should have know that something was wrong. The tall trees and thick brush seemed cold and lifeless. The whole area was dark and strange. Which was kind of odd, because the day was sunny and warm.

I cupped my hands around my mouth. "Angela!" I shouted into the forest. "Angela?!?!? Are you around here?!?!?"

No answer. Not a sound came from the dense, wooded thicket.

Conner and I jumped over the drainage ditch. It's about three feet wide, and, three feet deep. When it rains, the ditch fills up with water and runs off. It hadn't rained in several days, so today there wasn't much water in the ditch at all.

I raised my hands and cupped them around my mouth. "Angela?!?!?" I called out again. "Where are you?

As we approached the trees, we were enveloped by shade. The darkness seemed to swallow us up, and the air instantly grew colder. I couldn't help feeling like we were walking into some strange world or something. It was a spooky sensation.

"Have you ever been here?" I asked Conner, looking around.

He shook his head. "Nope," he replied. "I can think of better places to hang out."

"Me too," I said, staring up at a gnarled, old, oak tree. "But, I imagine, Grumpy would probably like playing around in the woods. I'll bet he's here somewhere."

"He's probably rolling around in the mud as we speak," Conner said, smiling.

"Oh, don't say that," I grimaced. "Then I'll have to give him a bath before Mom and Dad come home. I'll have to—"

Conner suddenly grasped my arm.

"Shhhhhh," he whispered.

We stopped walking, and listened. In the distance, I could hear the rush of cars on the highway. A horn honked a long ways off, and an airplane buzzed somewhere high overhead.

I slowly nodded my head closer to Conner. *"What is it?"* I asked quietly. *"What did you hear?"*

Conner paused a moment, then answered. "Well," he said, a bit louder, "I guess it was nothing.

I just thought that I heard something, that's all. Something moving. It must have been my imagination."

The problem was, it *wasn't* his imagination, as we were about to find out.

■■■

The wooded area around the drainage ditch isn't very big. Sure, there are quite a few trees and shrubs in the small two-acre tract, but there really isn't any way you could get lost. In two minutes, you could walk through the woods and be back in the subdivision.

We walked along a dense path. I was becoming more and more worried by the minute. I was concerned about Grumpy, but I was more worried about Angela. It wasn't like her to just disappear like that.

"Do you think she went home?" Conner considered. "She doesn't seem to be anywhere around here." He stopped walking, and stood next to a big, dead tree stump. Blades of sunlight sliced through the trees, and I looked around. There wasn't any sign of Grumpy or Angela. Or anyone else, for that matter. No footprints, no sounds, nothing.

"No," I responded to Conner's question. "She would have told us. She wouldn't have gone home without letting us know."

Suddenly, a twig snapped on the other side of the stump. Conner jumped, and I did, too. Then I laughed.

"Gosh, we're both a bit jumpy in these woods," I said.

But Conner didn't hear a single word I said. He took several quick steps backward, and I noticed that he was shaking.

"Conner?" I said. "Conner . . . what's wrong?"

He was really trembling now, and he was trying to speak—but no sound came from his lips. He raised his hand to point, and I could see his arm shaking badly.

"Conner?!?!?" I said again. I was worried. There was something wrong with him.

I looked at the stump he was pointing at, and a surge of horror hit me like a truck. My heart stopped. My skin crawled. My hair stood on end.

The 'stump' that Conner was pointing at was not a stump at all— *it was a spider!*

It was a living, moving, live spider, the size of

a picnic table! It was black, and had long, sinewy legs. Glaring, shiny eyes, the size of bowling balls, focused intently on Conner and I. Two dagger-like fangs protruded from the spider's mouth.

And it *moved!* It began to move, slowly, cautiously, one leg at a time—toward us!!

5

I've seen science fiction movies before, and I've seen some pretty scary, gross movies, too.

But this was no movie, and the terror I felt was ten times worse than any movie I've ever seen. A *thousand* times worse.

"Don't budge a muscle," Conner managed to whisper. His lips barely moved. "Maybe he can't see us."

I didn't tell Conner, but I couldn't have moved if I tried! I was too horrified by what I was seeing. It couldn't be real! Somehow, this had to be someone's idea of a joke. Probably my brother, Scott.

But then again, I knew this was no joke. I knew that we were looking at a real, honest-to-goodness spider. How it was possible, I didn't know. I didn't know what kind it was, and I didn't care. All I knew was that we were in *big* trouble.

Looking back, I don't think it would have mattered if we'd tried to run. Spiders are incredibly fast, as we were about to find out.

The huge, black creature seemed to be stalking us, creeping slowly forward, coming closer and closer. Conner was in the creature's path. I had managed to back up a few feet down the trail, away from the monstrous spider.

"Conner!" I gasped. "We have to get away! We have to run!"

The spider took another step toward Conner. Conner suddenly turned to flee—but it was too late.

All at once, a sticky, stringy substance shot through the air like lightning, striking Conner on the shoulder. When he tried to wipe it away, his hand stuck to it.

"Hey!" he shouted. "What's—"

He didn't have time to finish his words. In the

blink of an eye he was covered with a white, sticky, stringy web.

The spider was wrapping him up!

"Leah!" he panicked, as strands of web began to cover his mouth and face. "Leah! Help me! *HELP ME!!*"

In a flash, the spider was upon him. The hideous creature grasped Conner with three of its claw-like legs, spinning him around, wrapping him in silky-white webbing. There was nothing I could do to help my friend. It was a horrible, gut-wrenching feeling, knowing that I couldn't help Conner.

The only thing I could do was run. I could run, and try and get help. I would run all the way to the police station if I had to. Maybe it wouldn't be too late to save Conner.

Maybe.

But then again, maybe it was . . . because when I turned to flee down the path, I was face-to-face with *another* spider!

This one was even bigger than the one that had attacked Conner! It was brown and hairy with six eyes. Legs as thick as telephone poles methodically raised and lowered as the spider walked toward me. Branches snapped and cracked, and the gargantuan creature approached.

And then, I too, was hit by the strange, silky webbing. I tried to wipe it away, but my hand stuck to it! More of the gooey material hit me, and I tried wiping it off with my other hand. It stuck, too!

I let out a scream. It was loud, long, and shrill. I screamed with everything I had, hoping that someone would hear.

The spider lunged, and, in an instant, was upon me. Strong legs picked me up in the air, and at once I was spinning, tossed round and round. The white stringy web bound my legs, my hands and arms. It covered my eyes, my nose, my face. The only thing I could see were the shiny strands of web that were covering my eyes. I couldn't move an inch.

Then, everything began to go dark. Everything suddenly went black, and I passed out.

But that wasn't the worst of it—because the worst was yet to come.

6

Darkness. That's all I could see.

If you could call it *seeing*.

There was no light anywhere. Not a single, tiny glow. The air was stale and dry, and I was confused and disoriented. What had happened? Where was I?

I couldn't move. I was bound tightly by something, and my arms were frozen to my body. I felt like a mummy, bandaged firmly in soft, sticky cloth.

What had happened? Where was I? Why couldn't I move?!?!?

Then it all came back to me.

The spiders! The enormous, terrifying, ugly spiders at the drainage ditch had attacked, wrapping Conner and I in tight, webbed cocoons!

I was amazed to be alive. I was sure that when the spider was twirling me around and encasing me in webbing, I was a goner. I didn't remember fainting, but I was surprised that I actually woke up!

I didn't feel any pain, either. Whatever had happened to me, I hadn't been hurt.

Not yet, anyway.

I opened my mouth to cry for help. The webbing stuck to my lips and chin. A piece of the stringy substance caught under my bottom lip. It tasted dry and bitter. I was just about to shout—to scream and cry out for help—but I caught myself.

What if the huge spiders were nearby? What if they heard my cries for help? What would happen then? Sure, I was trapped, but at least I was *alive*. I didn't want to do anything that would make the spiders do something drastic.

But what would I do? What *could* I do? I was bound too tightly to move, but I couldn't just wait for help to arrive. Mom and Dad would be working till eight o'clock—but right now, I had no idea what time it was. I had fainted, and I might have been unconscious for hours . . . or *days!* The thought was chilling. But if it was still Friday, the same afternoon, then Mom and Dad wouldn't even know I was missing until tonight. By then, it might be too late. Spiders have to eat sometime, you know.

It was a horrible, horrible thought.

I tried real hard, and I managed to wriggle my toes in my shoes. After a few minutes of struggling, I was able to move my fingers a tiny bit. I found that if I pinched a tiny amount of the sticky web between my fingers, I could tear it away. It felt sticky and gooey, like cotton candy on a hot summer day. But if I slowly picked at the webbing with my fingers, perhaps I could slowly work a hole in the cocoon.

Maybe . . . just *maybe* . . . I could free myself.

I worked at it for a few minutes, but I wasn't making much progress. The process was terribly slow. The gum-like webbing kept getting stuck between my fingers, and it was tough to pull tiny pieces away and roll them into a ball.

It would take an entire day to work a hole in the cocoon, if I could even do it at all! Besides . . . I had no idea how thick the cocoon might be. It could be four feet thick for all I knew!

As time went by, my optimism faded, and my fear began to grow. I was slowly coming to terms with the fact that I was going to be spider food.

But when? How soon?

Questions whirled through my mind. Where had the spiders come from? Why hadn't they been spotted before? Are they really spiders—or some other weird, prehistoric creatures?

No, I thought. They're spiders, alright. I'd know a spider when I saw one, that was for sure.

And suddenly, in the inky blackness, I heard a noise. A faint scraping and shuffling.

Like . . . *legs.*

Spider legs.

My heart hammered in my chest. I took rapid, quick breaths. My horror was so great, I couldn't have screamed if I tried. Again, I struggled to move, but it was no use.

Then—

A tearing sound! The cocoon was being torn open! The spider was coming for me!!

The noise was awful. It sounded like a razor blade tearing through a paper bag. I could only imagine what was making that terrible noise.

Spider food, I thought. *This is it. I'm going to be a spider snack!*

I tried to struggle free, using all of my strength and energy, but it was no use.

I was right, and I knew it. Spider food. That's what I was going to be. An appetizer for an arachnid. A tasty treat for a terrible tarantula. In my mind, I could see the spider's glossy, black eyes, glaring hungrily at me. I could imagine huge knife-like fangs tearing into me, chewing me into a thousand pieces.

Another tear ripped at the cocoon, and then I *did* scream. Long and loud. My shriek probably didn't go far, but I didn't care. I panicked.

"Nooooooo!" I cried at the top of my lungs. *"Noooooooo! Help me!! Someone!!"*

And, at that moment, the cocoon was split open by a large, sharp claw.

It was all over! I was about to be devoured!

7

The claw ripped open the final layer of webbing. I thought about trying to run, trying to flee, but I knew that it would be no use. The spider would be upon me in seconds.

Besides . . . where would I run to? I didn't even know where I was!

I could hear the awful claw shredding the web cocoon. In seconds, I would feel it tearing into me. I was sure of it.

Suddenly — a voice!

"Leah! Shhhh!!"

Huh? That was no spider! That sounded like
. . . like . . . *Conner!*

"Conner?!?!?" I gasped. "Is . . . is that you?!?"

"No, it's Humpty-Dumpty!" Conner mocked.
"Of course it's me!"

The web casing tore away. I could see! It was
still kind of dark, but I could make out Conner's
shadowy form standing before me. He held a
pocketknife in his hand.

"How did you get away?" I asked.

"I was able to work one of my arms free and
reach the knife in my pocket," he replied, showing me
the blade. "It took me a few minutes, but I was finally
able to cut a hole in this stuff."

I struggled out of the opening Conner had
made in the cocoon, and he helped me out. "I was
able to tear a hole big enough to escape," he
continued. "I have no idea where we are. Are you
okay?"

"I . . . I guess so," I stammered. "Scared to
death, but I'm okay."

I looked around in the gloom. We were in
some sort of cave or tunnel. The air was thick and
damp, and reeked of mildew.

"Where are we?" I asked.

Conner turned and nodded at our dark, murky surroundings. It was like we were standing inside some big, round pipe. "Best I can tell," he began, "we're underground somewhere. But I haven't had much time to figure it out. As soon as I escaped, I saw a gray cocoon not far away. I was hoping that it was you. I'm glad you're okay."

"Let's get out of here," I pressed. "Let's get out of here . . . *now.*"

But another thought suddenly struck me like a bolt of lightning.

"Angela!" I exclaimed. "Oh no! What if she's here, too?!?! What if the spiders captured her?!?! That might be why she didn't come back to my house!"

"We've got to find her and get out of here," Conner said bravely. At least, he *sounded* brave. I, myself, wasn't feeling so brave at the moment.

But Conner was right. We couldn't leave without Angela. She was my best friend. One of my best friends, at least.

And best friends help their best friends. *Always.*

I looked around, trying to get my bearings. It

was impossible to imagine where we were. Where had the spiders taken us? How far were we from home? I had no answers.

"Come on," Conner urged. He took a deep breath. "We have to move. I think the spiders are gone, but sooner or later, they are going to come back. I don't want to be here when they do."

He grasped my hand, and we began walking. The ground beneath my feet was smooth and slimy. Slippery. We would have to be careful.

At least we could see where we were going. Not very well, but there seemed to be a tiny bit of light coming from somewhere.

In a moment, we knew where the light was coming from.

"Conner! Look!" I whispered. My arm shot out, and I pointed.

Ahead of us, a tiny light bulb glowed! It came from the wide, round tunnel. The light wasn't very bright at all, but just seeing it filled me with hope.

Maybe we would get out of here, after all!

Conner walked into the tunnel, and I followed. Suddenly, he froze. He stopped so quickly that I bumped into him. I peered around his shoulder.

"What is it?" I asked quietly. He raised his

hand to silence me. We stood motionless, staring down the long tunnel.

Then, I heard it. A scraping noise. It wasn't too far from where we were. The passageway split away right near the light bulb. The tunnel we were in kept going, but right beneath the light, a tunnel went to the left, and one to the right. The noise seemed to be coming from one of the two side passages.

Could it be Angela? Maybe she had escaped on her own! Maybe she was looking for us!

But I quickly found out that it wasn't Angela.

Suddenly, a thick, muscular leg appeared. Then another. They were large, fat legs, like tree trunks.

They were the legs of a giant spider — *and it was only a few feet away from us!*

The legs slowly emerged from the side tunnel, and, within seconds, the hulking body of the spider was directly in front of us.

But it didn't see us! Conner and I stood in the middle of the tunnel, frozen by fear, motionless. My breath stolen, I could do nothing but watch the gruesome creature pass directly in front of us. The gargantuan spider slowly made his way beneath the light . . . and into another tunnel! He hadn't spotted us!

As the spider disappeared into the opposite tunnel, I let out a sigh of relief. Soon, the spider was out of sight, and we could no longer hear him moving.

"That was close," whispered Conner.

"Where did they come from?" I asked. "Have they *always* been here?"

"You got me," Conner replied quietly. "I don't even know where we are. But, like I said, I think we're underground."

Conner was probably right. We appeared to be in some sort of huge, cement pipe. Maybe we were in some of the drainage pipes that run beneath Saginaw. Maybe they were sewer tunnels. Who knows.

What I did know for certain, however, was that as long as we were down here, we were in *real* danger.

But we weren't leaving yet. Not until we found Angela. Not until she was safe.

If it wasn't already too late.

"Let's go," I stated, urging Conner forward.

We started out carefully, quietly. The hard cement beneath our feet was slimy and slippery, and our steps were short and cautious.

When we reached the small, glowing light, we

stopped. I looked around.

We were definitely inside some sort of cement pipe. The walls were rounded, covered with a wet, green, algae-like substance. The watery, lime-colored walls shined like polished varnish.

Conner looked up at a small, steel plate beneath the light bulb. There were letters stamped into the metal. He leaned closer, gazing at the chiseled lettering.

"Saginaw Water Works," he read aloud. "So that's it! We *are* beneath the city! This is too bizarre!"

I peered down into one of the dark tunnels that went off to my left—the tunnel where we had seen the spider emerge. The tunnel opened up into a larger cavern. It was dark and dismal, but I could see shadows and . . . .

"Conner!" I hissed frantically. *"Look!"*

In the gloomy darkness, I could see a blurry, white glow. There was a faint, oblong form in the cavern!

"It's a cocoon!" Conner said. "It's one of those sticky things that *we* were wrapped up in!"

My hopes soared. *Was it Angela?!?! Could it really be her?!?!*

We set out down the tunnel, approaching the

45

cocoon cautiously. There wasn't much light, and it was difficult to see. I sure hoped that there weren't any spiders waiting in the shadows for us!

We reached the cocoon, and Conner pulled out his knife.

"Wait," I whispered quietly. Conner paused, holding the knife.

"Angela?" I asked quietly, speaking toward the large, fuzzy bundle. "Is that you?"

Suddenly, we could hear Angela's voice!"

"Leah?!?!? Oh my gosh!! Is that *you?!?!*" Her voice was muffled, and she sounded far away. But it was Angela, alright.

Angela was inside the cocoon!

"Yes!" I cried. "It's me! And Conner! We're okay!"

Conner carefully tore open the cocoon with his knife.

"Hang on just a second," I instructed Angela. "We'll get you out."

In moments, Conner had ripped open the cocoon. Angela escaped, slipping through the large slit that Conner had made with his knife.

"We found you!" I piped.

"I thought I was a goner for sure!" she

exclaimed.

"So did we," Conner replied. "This is the freakiest thing in the world!"

I helped peel the gooey, white webbing that still stuck to Angela's shirt and pants.

"Where are we?" she asked, rubbing her eyes as she gazed around at our strange surroundings. We began walking slowly back toward the light in the tunnel.

"As far as we can tell," Conner replied, "we're beneath the city. In some sort of drain tunnel or something."

"I have a suggestion," Angela offered. "How about us getting out of here as fast as we can?"

"Good suggestion," I agreed. "But right now, we're not exactly sure how to get out. We're not sure—"

I stopped speaking, and held my words in my mouth. Once again, fear washed over me like a tidal wave.

Because in the tunnel, coming right toward us, was an enormous black widow spider!

9

Angela screamed, and Conner quickly placed his hand over her mouth. He pulled her back into the dark tunnel, and I quickly followed.

"*Shhhhh,*" he cautioned. "*Maybe he didn't see us. Maybe he doesn't know we're here.*"

We ducked back into the side tunnel. Conner leaned forward, peering around the corner at the spider.

I crossed my fingers. The spider . . . if he kept crawling along the tunnel . . . would pass right in front of us! He would be only a few feet away!

But there was nothing else we could do. It was too dangerous to run, and if the spider spotted us, he'd catch us in a heartbeat. The only thing we could do was wait—and hope that we hadn't been discovered.

I held my breath. I was so scared I was trembling. Angela held her hands over her eyes, not wanting to see. Conner held out his pocketknife like a swordsman ready for battle. Not that a pocketknife would be much of a help, but there certainly wasn't anything else he could defend himself with.

Soon, a leg appeared. Then another, and another. The black widow was right in front of us, moving along the tunnel. We could hear its long, wiry legs scraping against the cement. I held my fingers tightly together, hoping.

Please, I thought. *Please keep going. Please keep going down the tunnel. Don't stop. Don't come this way. Just . . . keep . . . going . . . .*

We'd been able to hide from one spider already, and I hoped that our luck would continue. I wanted nothing more than to get out of here, away from horrible freaks of nature that had captured us and brought us to this awful place.

The enormous body of the spider came into view. It was huge! The creature's head was bigger than a beach ball. Its body was even bigger—much bigger.

And then, the spider did exactly what I was hoping it *wouldn't* do.

It stopped.

It turned.

It was looking right at us! Its' face—if you could call it a face—was hideous. I'd seen spiders close-up before, but there was nothing that could compare to the freakish creature that was before us.

My knees wobbled and my lip trembled. Blood pumped through my veins like little locomotives. Even Conner, who had been so brave a second ago, dropped his knife in disbelief.

I couldn't blame him.

The spider, slowly, so very slowly, began to move.

Our luck had just ran out.

10

I had never felt so helpless in my life. I guess I've always felt, no matter what, I'd be able to get out of any jam I got into. Plus, Mom and Dad would always take care of me. I always figured that, no matter what, I'd be okay.

I didn't feel that way anymore.

Mom and Dad weren't around. They had no idea that I was in danger. And there was no way that Angela, Conner, and I could defend ourselves from the dreadful creature before us.

The barbaric monster raised a huge, clawlike leg. It swept the air, just inches in front of us, then stopped. The giant spider, as well as the three of us, remained frozen.

And then— *the spider began to change!*

It was slow at first, but the spider began to shift and waver. It looked like he was growing *smaller!*

But there was more to it than that. The spider was actually changing *shape!*

Its' form was changing!

I reached down to pinch my arm. *I'm dreaming,* I told myself. *There is no way this is happening.* I grabbed a piece of skin and pinched hard to wake myself up.

"Ouch!" Angela shouted.

Whoops. Wrong arm.

Before us, the spider was now almost unrecognizable. Legs were disappearing, and the creature seemed to be shrinking. Its figure had changed so much that he no longer even looked like a spider. In fact, he began to look like . . . like . . . *a human!*

It was! The spider was changing into human form!

I took a step back. Angela followed, then

Conner, who had forgot all about his knife that had clanged to the cement floor. He was paying attention to the spider — or whatever it was — in front of us in the tunnel.

The form became more recognizable. A human nose, ears, and legs — sort of. The 'skin' if you could call it that — still looked like it belonged to a spider. But the shape of the creature was now definitely human.

And when it spoke, I just about fainted for the *second* time that day. It spoke in a voice so human and friendly that I couldn't believe it.

But what blew me away was the fact that I *recognized the voice!* I'd heard that voice before!

Just what — or *who* — was it?

"Don't be frightened," the creature said.

I just about fell out of my skin!

The voice! That was the voice of Jarred Rook! I go to school with Jarred! He's one of my classmates!

But that was impossible! How could Jarred Rook be one of these . . . these *creatures* . . . whatever they were?!?!

Seeing our expressions of horror, Jarred spoke again.

"It's okay," he assured us calmly. "It's just me.

Jarred."

And it was! It really was—sort of. His face, neck and hands had human skin, but the rest of his body was kind of shiny and black, like plastic. His body still had the texture of a spider, but he was shaped like a human being. Not to be rude, but he was pretty strange looking.

"I know this looks really weird," he agreed, "but I guess you know now."

Conner, Angela, and I were speechless. We didn't know what to say. We could only stand there, dumbfounded, staring at Jarred Rook. I couldn't believe that he was one of my *classmates!*

Conner spoke first. "What do you mean?" he asked Jarred.

"Now you know," Jarred reiterated, a smile coming to his lips. "I'm an arachno-sapien."

"An arachno-*what?*" I asked. I'd never heard of such a thing.

"An arachno-sapien," Jarred repeated. "I'm half-human, half-spider."

Half-human and half-spider! That's crazy!

I was still in a state of disbelief, but then I began to grow angry. After all, we had been kidnapped! All three of us! That's illegal!

"Why did you capture us?!?!" I demanded. "Why did you bring us down here?!?!"

"Yeah!" Angela hammered, her anger growing. "You just about scared me to death!"

Jarred Rook shook his head. "That wasn't us," he explained. "That wasn't us at all."

"Us?!?!" Conner asked. "Who do you mean by 'us'?"

"The arachno-sapiens," Jarred answered. "But please . . . let me start at the beginning."

I'd already been freaked out beyond belief several times today . . . but it was nothing like the bombshell I received when Jarred told me his unbelievable story . . . .

"First of all," Jarred began, "you need to know that all arachno-sapiens are peaceful. We don't hurt anyone. I promise. We're people, just like you . . . only we can change into spiders whenever we want to."

"You mean like *Spider-Man?*" Conner asked.

"Well, sort of," Jarred acknowledged, nodding his head. "Except that we arachno-sapiens have the ability to change completely into spiders, as you've seen. And besides . . . *Spider-Man* is a cartoon. We're *real."*

A chill ran down the middle of my back. Last summer, when we vacationed on Mackinac Island, I met a girl who showed me a stone with a dragonfly carved in it. She claimed she had been able to fly with the stone! She said her younger brother had a stone with a spider carved into it, and he had been able to climb like a spider when he carried the stone. I thought that they were kooks!

They didn't seem so strange anymore.

"We arachno-sapiens came from another planet, long ago," Jarred continued. "Our peaceful home had been attacked by a renegade band of creatures known as octogores. In essence, octogores are simply spiders — huge ones, that is. But they were stronger and more powerful than we arachno-sapiens. We were forced to leave our planet and flee to safety. We came here, to earth, where we could blend in with humans without anyone knowing."

"But how come no one knows about you?" I asked. "If you don't want to harm anyone, why the big secret?"

"Sometimes humans do silly things," Jarred replied, rolling his eyes. "Because we're different, we decided to keep our secret from humans. Besides . . . many humans would be terrified of us, and would never understand."

"This is like something from the *X Files*," Conner breathed.

Jarred laughed. "You, as a human, might think that," he chuckled. "But we, as arachno-sapiens, know that we are real. Actually, there are several hundred of us that live in and around Saginaw. I'm sure you've met a few arachno-sapiens, but you just don't know it. We are pretty quiet about our secret."

I had read somewhere that the truth was often stranger than fiction. Now I knew what that statement meant.

"The octogores followed us here," Jarred continued. "They began arriving last summer. They stay down here, below the city, keeping out of sight in the sewer pipes and drain systems."

"Why are they here?" I asked. "I mean, if they can travel to other planets and stuff, why did they come here, to earth? To Saginaw?"

Jarred took a deep breath and looked into my eyes. Then he glanced at Conner, then at Angela.

"The octogores have discovered a way to poison all of the humans on this planet—and turn every single person alive—into spiders," Jarred explained, his voice full of concern. "Only, once a human has been transformed into a spider, the octogores plan on using them as their slaves. That's why they've come to earth. You . . . and everyone on your entire planet . . . are in grave danger."

"You mean . . . that's what captured us?" Conner asked. "One of those . . . those *octogores?*"

Jarred nodded his head. "They didn't harm you, because they want to wait until their plan is set. Then they would have turned you into spiders, and you would have been their slaves."

Talk about being freaked out! My palms sweated, and my heart clanged noisily in my chest.

Spiders?!?! Slaves?!?! Impossible!

But, seeing *is* believing, and I had just witnessed one of the most bizarre things I'd ever seen in my life. I'd believe just about anything right about now.

"There's just—" Jarred began to speak, but he stopped in mid-sentence.

A scraping noise echoed from down the tunnel. We all turned our heads.

Legs suddenly appeared from a side tunnel. More legs. Brown, hairy legs. *Huge* legs.

"Uh-oh," Jarred whispered, and I knew right away that the spider that was coming wasn't an arachno-sapien.

It was an octogore — and something told me he wasn't dropping by to say 'hello'!

The enormous spider faced us. He was so big that he had to bend his legs to fit inside the cavern.

And he was *ugly*. Eyes the size of bowling balls glistened menacingly in the dim light. Two large fangs protruded from an open, gaping mouth. He was ghastly, and he slowly began to crawl toward us.

"Move back!" Jarred ordered. "Get into the side tunnel!"

The three of us did as he instructed, hunkering down into the shadows.

Instantly, Jarred began to change again! He was morphing—changing back into a spider! In seconds he had grown huge, with long, black legs. Jarred Rook looked just like a six-foot tall black widow spider!

Suddenly, the octogore lunged at Jarred. Jarred—now a spider once again—lashed out with his long, powerful legs, fending off the charging brown octogore. For a moment it felt like Conner, Angela and I had shrunk, and that we were watching two normal-sized spiders fight. Like somehow, *we* were the ones that were strange, because we were so small. It was an eerie feeling.

The two spiders continued to battle. The octogore's long, piercing fangs chomped furiously. Its long, strong legs tried to grasp Jarred.

But Jarred was too quick, too limber. He expertly blocked each one of the octogore's legs, knocking them away as fast as the hideous creature could attack.

Suddenly, a stream of webbing shot out from Jarred! It stuck to the brown spider, and Jarred kept it coming. The octogore tried to push away the sticky gray webbing, but Jarred was too fast. Within seconds, the brown spider's legs were bound tightly.

The octogore struggled, but it couldn't move.

Jarred continued wrapping the spider in webbing, encasing the struggling monster in a cotton-like ball. The ball was enormous — almost as wide as the tunnel itself!

Jarred, still very much a spider, easily rolled the large ball down the tunnel and into a side cavern.

I must admit, watching the whole battle had been pretty freaky — but it was kind of cool, too.

Jarred crawled back toward us. As he did, he began morphing back into human form. In seconds, he looked human again.

Well . . . *almost* human.

"There are more than I thought," he explained, after changing back into the 'normal' Jarred Rook that I knew.

"What's going to happen now?" I asked him.

"Well, now that you know about us, we could really use your help," Jarred said.

"Help?!?!" Angela asked. "What can *we* do? We can't fight these Octo-whatevers!"

"And you shouldn't," Jarred warned sharply. "They're too dangerous. But I need to get a message to someone who can help. Another arachno-sapien."

"Hey," Conner offered, "I'll take a message to

the Queen of Egypt if I have to." He looked around. "I just want out of these tunnels!"

"You'll have to move fast," Jarred said. "I can help you get out of here, but you need to find Mr. Emerson as quickly as possible."

My jaw hit the floor.

"Mr. Emerson?!?!?" Angela and I both chimed. *"Our science teacher?!?!?"*

Jarred nodded. "Yes," he replied, "Mr. Emerson is an arachno-sapien. He is in terrible danger."

"Mr. Emerson?!?!?" I asked again. "Why? What do the octogores want with Mr. Emerson?"

"Mr. Emerson has developed a formula that causes the octogores to freeze," Jarred explained. "He calls it 'acid-ice', and he discovered it by accident. All you have to do is spray an octogore with the acid-ice, and it will cause the spider to freeze instantly. Then, the spider will crumble and turn to dust. Now that Mr. Emerson has invented acid-ice, the octogores will stop at nothing to get it from him."

"Well, if this 'acid-ice' works so well, how come *you're* not using it?" Angela quizzed.

Jarred bobbed his head. "Oh, believe me, I will," Jarred answered. "Mr. Emerson just finished pouring the acid-ice into small spray cans. They are locked in his safe in his laboratory at the school. He planned on using the cans when we found the nest."

"The nest?" I asked. "What nest?"

Jarred's face grew tense, his eyes serious. "We know that the octogores have made a nest somewhere," he explained. "They've laid eggs . . . thousands of them . . . somewhere. We just don't know where they are. We've been hunting for the nest for weeks. Every single arachno-sapien is searching for the nest right now, before the eggs hatch into tiny octogores. If they hatch, there is no way we'll be able to stop them. There will be too many."

My hopes faded, and my horror grew. Seeing my expression of stark terror, Jarred spoke again.

"But there's still time," he offered hopefully. "The poison hasn't started to flow . . . yet. There's a special tank at the water plant that is filled with the poison. When the plant begins to operate, the octogores will open a valve, allowing the liquid to mix with the clean water. You won't be able to taste the poison, but it will be there. If that tainted water just touches the lips of a human, they will become a spider within twenty-four hours. I'm staying here, in the tunnels beneath the city, to try and stop more octogores from entering the water plant—and to look for the nest. What you need to do is get the message to Mr. Emerson. Tell him that the octogores are going to use the new water tower. He'll know what to do from there."

It sounded simple enough. If that's all we had to do, our mission would be a piece of cake.

We followed Jarred as he walked through the wide tunnel. We made turn after turn, and it seemed like we had walked for miles. These large pipes seemed to criss-cross beneath the entire city.

Finally, we came to a place where a door opened up. Jarred unbolted a lock, and we squinted in the bright sunlight.

"Hey!" Conner said, looking around. "I know where we are! This is the hill on the other side of the grocery-mart on Ash street!"

"Right," Jarred said. "The door is built into the hill. There are many ways to access the tunnels, but this one is the closest to Mr. Emerson's home. Quick! Go!"

And with that, Jarred climbed back into the tunnel and slammed the steel door closed behind him.

Mr. Emerson lives on Ash street. I've biked by his home a few times, and once in a while I've seen him outside washing his car or working in the yard. We could run to his house in two minutes. Simple.

Unfortunately, our simple plan was about to go haywire.

14

The three of us tore through a vacant field and sprinted down the street. I'm a pretty fast runner—faster than Conner and Angela, anyway—but all three of us ran together just to be safe. We were at Mr. Emerson's house in no time, and we didn't waste a second. We dashed right up to the front door of his house.

I banged on the door with my fist. "Mr. Emerson!" I shouted. "Mr Emerson? Are you home?"

Silence. Behind the door we heard nothing.

"Maybe he's not home," Angela wondered aloud.

I pounded the door again. "Mr. Emerson?"

We waited for a moment, then we heard a shuffling sound. Whew! Mr. Emerson was coming to the door!

But we were in for a surprise.

"Can I help you?" a strange voice asked from behind the closed door.

"Mr. Emerson?" I said. "It's me . . . Leah Warner."

"Mr. Emerson doesn't live here anymore," the voice replied flatly. "I'm sorry. Please go away."

Huh? That didn't make any sense! Mr. Emerson has *always* lived at this house!

I was about to speak when Conner held up his hand to silence me. He placed a finger to his lips, urging me to keep quiet.

What was he thinking?

"Okay," Conner said loudly, answering the voice behind the door. "Sorry to bother you." He glanced at Angela and I, nodded to us, and turned, stepping off the porch. He mouthed the words *'come on'*, and strode across the yard. We followed, walking behind him as he made his way to the sidewalk.

I shot a quick glance over my shoulder and saw a white curtain flutter inside Mr. Emerson's house. Whoever was there had been watching us!

"Come on," Conner whispered, walking away from Mr. Emerson's home. "Don't look back. Just keep walking. I think Mr. Emerson is in trouble."

"Then why are we walking away?" Angela asked quietly.

"Because whoever — or *whatever* — is in Mr. Emerson's house, they were watching us. We need to make him think that we're leaving. Then, we can sneak back around the other side of the house and look in the windows."

After we were a safe distance from the house, we crossed through two backyards and emerged on the other side of the block. From there, we walked down the street. Soon, Mr. Emerson's home came into view.

"Perfect," Conner whispered quietly, scanning the surroundings. "There are a lot of trees and shrubs in the neighbor's yard. We can creep up to the back of Mr. Emerson's house without being spotted by whoever is inside."

"I don't know," I said, shaking my head slowly.

"Maybe we should tell someone. Like the police."

"Uh-huh," Conner chided, rolling his eyes. "And what do you think the police are going to say when you tell them that giant spiders are attacking the city of Saginaw? They'll toss you in the looney-bin."

Conner was right, of course. No one on earth would believe what we'd just seen. We would have to get the message to Mr. Emerson ourselves.

"Okay," I reluctantly agreed.

We sneaked through backyards and had to jump a fence. I caught the pant-leg of my jeans and tore them, but I hardly noticed. Considering what was at stake, a tear in my jeans didn't seem to matter much.

Finally, we came to Mr. Emerson's house. Everything seemed to be fine. The sun was still shining, and blue jays were splashing in a bird-bath in Mr. Emerson's yard. Bumblebees buzzed around a blooming apple tree, and several doves sat quietly on a fence, eyeing us suspiciously. Things seemed perfectly normal—until we heard Mr. Emerson's faint screams coming from inside his house!

We could just barely hear the shouts, but it was Mr. Emerson, alright. I was positive.

We crept up below the kitchen window. Mr. Emerson's voice was stronger now, and we could make out what he was saying.

"You will never succeed!" he proclaimed loudly. "Never! I will see to that!"

"We can, and we will," a strange voice rasped. "Now that we have you, there's nothing anyone can do to stop us!"

It was the same voice that we'd heard at the front door!

Slowly, I peered up above the window sill. Conner, on my left, and Angela, on my right, did the same.

If my eyes could have popped out of their sockets and fell to the floor, they would have—right then and there.

It was Mr. Emerson, alright—but he was sitting in a chair with his hands tied behind his back!

But that wasn't the worst of it.

In front of Mr. Emerson were two huge spiders!

Octogores! Both were dark brown and had huge, menacing eyes. Their legs had light brown rings around them. In a word, they looked *repulsive*. I mean . . . I hate spiders as it is . . . even the little bitty ones! I had a hard time just thinking that my friend, Jarred Rook, was half-human, half-spider!

Mr. Emerson didn't look frightened, though. He looked angry.

"What are we going to do now?" Angela whispered.

"We have to help Mr. Emerson somehow," I answered quietly.

But how?

"Maybe we can kill them with a big can of bug killer," Conner suggested.

I rolled my eyes. *"Spiders aren't bugs,"* I whispered. *"It's too bad we don't have any of that acid-ice that Jarred was talking about."*

We had been standing on our tip-toes, when Conner slowly lowered his heels to the ground. As he did, a twig beneath his foot snapped! The sound wasn't very loud . . . but it was loud enough to draw the attention of the two octogores inside the house!

"Great!" I hissed. *"Now you've done it!"*

Like lightning, the two giant spiders charged the sliding glass door. It slid open with a bang, and before we even had a chance to run, the octogores were upon us, enormous legs outstretched, baring their sharp, vicious teeth!

16

There was no time for an escape, and there was nothing we could do. The octogores struck so quickly we barely had a chance to breathe! They instantly snared all three of us with their strong, long legs. I'll tell you . . . it's no use trying to fight off a creature that has eight legs — especially when the legs are as big around as tree trunks!

I screamed, but we were dragged into Mr. Emerson's home so quickly that no one outside would have been able to hear. The sliding glass door slammed closed behind us.

Suddenly, one of the spiders spoke!

"He's gone!" he rasped angrily. "Where did he go?!?!?"

Mr. Emerson was no longer seated in the chair! The ropes that had bound his hands were on the floor, but Mr. Emerson was nowhere in sight.

"Find him!" the spider that clutched me wheezed. "We must find him!!"

I was still trying to struggle free, but it was no use. The giant octogore was just too strong.

The other spider had snared both Angela and Conner. They were squirming to get away, too—but they weren't having much luck. "Wrap them up!" the spider ordered.

"We don't have time!" snapped the other. "We must find him!"

Suddenly the spider that held me lunged forward. He carried me down the hall, opening a door with a single, huge, hairy claw. Behind the door, steps led down into a dark basement.

"Put them in here!" the spider ordered. "Hurry!"

Suddenly, I was thrust through the doorway. The spider let go of me and I fell, tumbling down the steps. I fell head over heels, smacking into the stairs, the wall, and finally, the hard cement floor.

"OOOOF!" I groaned as I hit the cold cement. Immediately, I leapt to my feet. My wrist was sore, and I would have some bruises from the tumble, but I was okay. I could have broken my neck!

In the next moment, Conner and Angela came flying down the steps. They plunged headlong, smacking into one another as they pitched over one another down the stairs. The door above slammed closed just as Conner and Angela smacked into me at the bottom of the steps, sending me flying like a bowling pin.

I bounced to my feet again. "Angela!" I cried. "Conner! Are you guys okay?"

Angela had a bloody nose, but it wasn't bad. Conner had a scraped elbow, but that was it. We were all lucky that we hadn't been hurt worse.

Boy . . . when Mom and Dad find out about these spiders, they're going to get it!

But, then again, it might be too late for Mom or Dad to help. They wouldn't be home till later tonight—and it was only mid-afternoon!

If they only knew.

"We've got to get out of here!" Conner

exclaimed. "We have to! We have to find Mr. Emerson and tell him about the water tower!"

A single window glowed from the other side of the basement. I ran to it, looking for a way to get it open. No luck. Even if we were able to open it, the window would still be too small for us to crawl through.

"This window doesn't open!" I cried. Conner ran to my side.

"Let's try and break it!" he said. "Maybe we can yell for help!"

On the floor was a monkey-wrench, and Conner snapped it up.

"Get back!" he ordered. He swung the wrench at the window.

BAM!

The window shuddered violently, but nothing happened!

BAM! BAM!

Still nothing!

"It must be plexiglass!" Conner exclaimed. Plexiglass is a lot like real glass, only it's made out of a clear plastic-like material. It's really strong, and it's almost impossible to break.

Conner swung again, harder this time.

BAM!

Still, nothing happened.

We were frantic. We had to get out of the basement quickly—but how?

Upstairs, on the other side of the door, we could hear voices and noises as the spiders searched frantically for Mr. Emerson. It didn't sound like they were having much luck. I could hear chairs being tossed about, a table tipping over, and other crashing sounds as the terrible octogores tried to find Mr. Emerson. After a few minutes, all was silent on the other side of the door.

I bounded up the steps and stood by the basement door, listening. I couldn't hear anything. Angela and Conner tip-toed up the stairs.

"I don't hear anything," I said quietly, shaking my head. "You want to try and get out?"

"As long as we don't have to deal with those over-grown daddy long-legs," Angela replied.

I tried the doorknob, but it was locked. I tried pushing on the door, but it wouldn't budge.

"Now what?" Conner asked.

I was looking down, when I noticed a slight movement. It came from beneath the door. Conner saw it, too.

"Ugh!" he croaked. "I've seen about enough of these things."

It was a small spider, about the size of a quarter. It was a light brown color. I'd seen a lot of spiders that looked like this one before.

Conner raised his foot to stomp on the spider.

"No!" I shouted, motioning him to stop. "Wait! Wait a second!"

Conner held his foot up in mid-air. He looked curiously at me, then down at the spider crawling out from beneath the door.

"What?" he asked. "What's the matter?"

"I'm not sure," I explained. "But . . . just wait a minute."

The tiny spider sat motionless on the floor, as if it was watching us.

And then—

Just when I thought things couldn't get any freakier, they did.

17

The spider began to grow! It doubled in size, then doubled again, then again!

It was getting *huge!!!*

Conner backed away and lowered his foot, and all three of us ran down the steps to the basement. The spider continued to grow . . . but now it was changing shape! Its features were becoming more and more human by the second—just like Jarred Rook had done!

We waited at the bottom of the steps, hoping

that it wasn't one of the octogores.

Human arms took shape, then legs and hands. And a face.

It was Mr. Emerson!

In less than a minute, the tiny spider had grown and morphed into Mr. Emerson! He stood at the top of the stairs in front of the closed door, looking down at us.

Boy, was I relieved! I thought we were goners!

Mr. Emerson raised a finger to his lips, urging us to be silent. *"Wait here,"* he whispered. *"Just remain quiet, and wait here."*

Of course, we were locked in the basement. We certainly weren't going anyplace very soon!

Instantly, Mr. Emerson began to change once again, and his features took the shape of a spider. He grew smaller and smaller, until he was no longer visible from where we stood.

Weird. Totally and completely *weird.*

Conner, Angela and I waited in silence. Seconds ticked past, then minutes. It was maddening.

Suddenly, the door clicked open and swung wide! Mr. Emerson stood at the top of the stairs. He was in human form again, only his legs and upper body still looked like he was part-spider. He raised his arm and urged us forward.

"Come up," he said. "They've gone. It's safe." We rushed up the steps and through the door.

The house was in shambles. Chairs had been strewn about, and even a couch in the living room had been tipped over. A magazine rack was broken, and a dozen newspapers and periodicals carpeted the floor.

"So," Mr. Emerson said, glancing at each one of us. "You three now know our secret."

We all nodded our heads. "Jarred Rook told us," I explained. "Below the city, in the tunnels. We had been captured by the octogores, but Jarred saved us."

"Nasty things," Mr. Emerson said, shaking his head.

"But how did you get away?" Angela asked. "We could hear two octogores searching your house for you."

"I morphed into a spider and shrunk myself down," Mr. Emerson explained. "Then I hid beneath the crack of the basement door. The octogores came in over here."

"You can do that?" Conner quizzed. "That's freaky!"

"All arachno-sapiens can shrink to much smaller sizes," he responded.

"I'm sure glad I didn't squish you," Conner said, offering a meek grin.

"Oh, you wouldn't have been able to," Mr. Emerson smiled. "You see, we retain one hundred percent of our strength, no matter what size we are. You couldn't have squished me if you tried. Besides," he continued, pointing to the floor, "I could have just darted beneath the door before your foot was even close to me."

"So, where have the octogores gone?" I asked.

"The same place that they think I escaped to," he replied. "Come."

We followed him across the living room and down the hall. At the end of the hallway stood a door that was open a tiny crack. Mr. Emerson swung it outward, and stepped back.

Stone steps led down into a dark tunnel. The walls of the tunnel were concrete, just like the passageway where the octogores had taken us!

"These steps lead into the pipes beneath the city," Mr. Emerson explained. "I built the steps when I first heard of the octogore invasion. I knew that we'd need a place to enter and leave the tunnels quickly. The two octogores have gone back into the tunnels."

Mr. Emerson closed the door and bolted it.

"Jarred said that you have a plan to stop them," Conner spoke up. "He told us to tell you that the octogores are going to use the new water tower and release their chemical into the city's water supply."

Mr. Emerson's eyes lit up, and he raised his gray eyebrows. "The new water plant!" he exclaimed. "I should have known! They'll release their serum into the water, and anyone who drinks it will turn into a spider! Everyone in the city of Saginaw will turn into spiders! They'll become slaves of the octogores!"

"Can't we stop them?" I asked. "Jarred said that you invented some kind of acid that will freeze the octogores."

"Yes," Mr. Emerson affirmed. "The acid-ice will stop the octogores. We have two problems, however. First, we must stop the octogores from releasing their poison into the water. Second, the cans of acid-ice are locked in the school laboratory. I'll have to retrieve them."

"But Jarred Rook said that the water tower is

scheduled to go into operation today," I stated.

On the kitchen table was a newspaper, and Mr. Emerson picked it up. He flipped through it, his eyes quickly scanning the pages. Suddenly, he gasped in horror!

"Oh no!" he exclaimed, glancing at a clock on the wall. "It's scheduled to open in an hour! The water will begin flowing to the city in one hour from now!"

Time was running out, and we needed to act quickly. We decided that Angela would go with Mr. Emerson to the science lab at school and help him retrieve the cans of acid-ice. Conner and I would rush to the new water plant to see if there was anything we could do. I didn't know exactly *what,* but maybe we'd have an idea when we got there.

"You should be fine," Mr. Emerson assured Conner and I. "Octogores usually stay in tunnels and dark places. They don't like to come out in the daylight unless they absolutely have to."

Unfortunately, we were about to find out otherwise.

18

Mr. Emerson's gray minivan was in the garage, and he and Angela leapt inside and whisked off, heading toward the school. Conner and I began running toward the new water plant.

"Do you think it's too late?" Conner huffed as we sprinted down the block.

"Hey, you've got me," I puffed back. "But I hope not. I *really* hope not."

We raced down the sidewalk, sprinted across a street, and bounded down another block. The air was dry, and the day was hot.

"Over there!" I pointed, still sprinting. "Let's cut across that field! It will be shorter than going all the way down the side streets to the main entrance!"

We turned and dashed across a yard, behind a big, stately home, and into the cluttered field. Large mounds of dirt had been piled up in many places, and there were pieces of heavy machinery—bulldozers, cranes, and the like—sitting idle in various places. A few months ago, road workers had started to develop the land. They're putting in a new subdivision and a new road with a couple bridges, but the area isn't open yet.

The new water plant sat far on the other side of the large meadow. An enormous, silver spire gleamed in the bright sunshine. The words SAGINAW were printed on the face of the new tower, some two hundred feet in the air. Below the tower sat a newly-built, three-story brick building. Sunlight reflected from the windows, and the appearance was peaceful and serene. It didn't seem possible that such horrific danger was less than one hour away.

Less than one hour away . . . unless we could stop the octogores.

Running through the field was tough. The

grass was tall, and there were large rocks that we had to look out for, as well as holes and ditches. The workmen had really ripped up the field in preparation for the new buildings. There were a few places that we couldn't run at all, for fear of tripping over something and breaking our necks.

We came to the edge of a very large ditch, and stopped. Bulldozers had been used to dig a large, crater-like hole. It was wide, too. At the bottom of the hole, a big cement drain pipe tucked into the wall of the crater. I knew in an instant that the pipe was connected to the underground drain system.

Where the octogores were.

"Let's go around," I instructed Conner. "I don't want to go anywhere near that drain pipe."

I crept carefully along the edge of the hole, eyeing the drain pipe suspiciously. The pit was big and dark, and I hated to think what was lurking in the tunnels beneath Saginaw. I could imagine a giant, hideous octogore sitting in the mouth of the tunnel at the bottom of the crevice, waiting, watching . . . hoping for something or someone like Conner or I to wander by. Just the thought of it creeped me out!

"Leah!" Conner suddenly shouted from behind me. *"Watch it! Watch out!"*

But it was too late. I had been walking, looking down at the drain pipe, and hadn't noticed the loose, unstable ground at the edge of the hole. The dirt below me suddenly fell away in clumps, and I lost my footing. It happened so quickly, there was no chance to do anything. The ground around us collapsed, and we plummeted, tumbling down the steep embankment to the bottom of the hole.

To the cement drain pipe.

19

Everything happened so fast that I didn't even have a chance to step back away from the edge of the hole. Conner had spotted the weak spot at the last moment and had turned back, but he had only succeeded in grasping at the loose dirt as the ground fell out from beneath him. He lost his grip and tumbled down the bank, landing next to me with a heavy thump.

A grain of sand stung my eye. A tear formed, washing it away. I jumped to my feet and brushed myself off. Conner did the same. "Nice going," he remarked sharply.

"Hey," I replied, about to explain that there was no way I could've known that the ground was unstable. "I didn't see—"

A sudden movement in the cement pipe caused me stop. My heart double-timed in my chest, and I began backing away toward the side of the hole.

"C . . . Conner," I stuttered. "Did . . . did you see that?"

"Uh-huh," he replied, clearly startled. We both backed up as far as we could.

Something in the wide, dark pipe moved again—something *big*—and I knew what it was. This was what I had imagined, what I feared. It would only make sense.

Hidden in the mouth of the tunnel was a giant spider.

An octogore.

"Do you think he's spotted us?" I whispered, my lips trembling.

"I don't know, and I don't care," Conner replied. *"Let's just get out of here."*

It was easier said than done. I turned slowly, keeping my eye on the drain pipe a dozen feet away, while I tried to climb out of the hole—which turned out to be impossible.

The problem was, the dirt crumbled away as we tried to take steps, and we couldn't climb anywhere. It was maddening. We could try all day, and the dirt would just fall back into the hole.

We were trapped.

Suddenly, I remembered a trick that I used to play on ants. That's right . . . *ants*. At the beach, I would make little craters in the sand with my finger. Then I'd catch an ant and place him in the hole. The ant would frantically try and scramble out, but the grains of sand wouldn't hold. The ant would spin his legs as fast as he could, but he'd never make any progress until I helped him out.

That's how I felt right now. Like a helpless, tiny ant, trying to scramble out of a sand crater.

Only there was no one around to help us out. Conner and I were stuck.

Over my shoulder, I saw another movement from the pipe, and it was all I could do to stifle a scream.

The octogore—the huge, grotesque creature that had been waiting inside the pipe—was coming out! A leg appeared out of the darkness, and then another. The creature moved slowly and methodically, like a cat stalking a bird.

Ghastly, glaring eyes glowed from the shadows. More legs emerged from the tunnel, and now the awful monster was in full view. Its eyes were a dark, obsidian black. The creature itself was a tanned brown, the color of autumn oak leaves. Large pincher-like claws were at the end of each leg, and I knew that with one snap of a single talon, the creature could tear us in half.

And when the spider suddenly lunged at us, I knew that there was nothing Conner or I could do.

20

I shrieked in horror as the giant creature charged, and Conner let out a screech that sounded like the squealing tires of a braking car. We both made one last, frantic attempt to climb the wall of the crater, but it was no use. The dirt just crumbled beneath our feet.

Perhaps, somehow, someway, I was being paid back for putting ants in little holes at the beach. The thought was awful.

If I ever get out of here, I thought, *I'll never place another ant in a single pit. Never.*

A spiny, jagged claw grasped my waist, and I yelped, struggling to break free. Another leg had snatched Conner. Both of us were instantly picked up off the ground, dangling in the air. I twisted furiously, trying to get away, but my efforts were in vain.

We were doomed!

But I noticed something. The spider held us firmly, but not tightly, as if it didn't want to hurt us. It began to climb the embankment, carefully holding us in the air.

Was it possible? Was this creature an arachno-sapien, and not an octogore?

Could we be that lucky?

The creature's legs were much better adapted to climbing than ours were, and the spider had no problem scaling up the dirt wall of the crater. In seconds, the giant spider had whisked us to the top of the hole.

Suddenly, Conner and I were on the ground again! The spider gently set us down on the ground and began backing down into the hole.

It *was* an arachno-sapien! It must have been! An octogore would have taken us and wound us up in webbing, but this creature had actually helped us!

Boy, was I sure glad about that!

"Did that just happen?" Conner breathed. We watched as the large spider slipped back into the dark tunnel.

"Come on," I said, looking across the field at the water tower. "We don't have much time left."

We made our way around the hole at a safe distance. I didn't want to go through that again!

White, cauliflower clouds tumbled in the blue sky above. The sounds of the city buzzed all around us as we jogged through the field, around more piles of dirt and equipment. We skirted several more large holes, wary of any places that an octogore might be hiding. *Next time,* I thought, *it might not be an arachno-sapien hiding in a drainage pipe. Next time, we might not be so lucky.*

The water plant was surrounded by a big, wire fence, and we followed it around to the front gate. The gate was open, and, while we watched, several cars and trucks came in and out.

"Look over there," Conner said. He pointed across a parking lot filled with cars and trucks.

Hundreds of people milled about. Most people were dressed nicely. Men wore suits and fancy ties. Women were equally well-dressed, and many people wore sunglasses to shield their eyes from the bright, late afternoon sun.

"What's going on?" I whispered. "Why are all of those people there?"

"You've got me," Conner replied. "Come on. Let's go find out."

We walked through the gate and into the parking lot. The crowd of people gathered near the front steps of the new building. Above, the huge water tower overshadowed the building.

Suddenly, I realized what was happening.

"Oh no!" I exclaimed in horror. "It's a ribbon-cutting ceremony! They're going to officially open the water plant after they cut the ribbon!"

We sprang into action—knowing that we may already be too late.

21

"A back door!" I panted to Conner as we ran around the parking lot to the other side of the building. "There has to be a back door! We have to get inside before they turn on the main water valves!"

There was a lot of laughter coming from the front of the building, and I guessed that everyone was focused on the celebration. Gravel crunched beneath my sneakers, and my lungs heaved. No one seemed to notice us as we ran around cars and trucks at the far edge of the parking lot.

Lucky for us, I thought. *If we're not too late.*

And, speaking of luck, there *was* a back door to the building! A large, gray, steel door provided the only entrance behind the building. Here, there were only a few windows—not near as many as there were at the front of the water plant.

"Come on!" I urged, racing up a cement walkway to the door. Conner's footsteps drummed behind me, and in moments we were at the door.

Please be open, I thought. *Oh, please . . . please be open.*

I hadn't had time to slow my run, and I literally slammed into the door. My hands grasped the thick, round knob.

Please be open . . . .

I twisted my hand, and the knob turned.

The door clicked open!

I couldn't believe it! I pulled the heavy door open and stepped inside. Conner followed, and he closed the door behind him.

We were in a wide hallway. Shiny, dark tile glowed beneath our feet. The walls were a crisp, creamy white, and there were three closed doors on each side of the hall. All of the doors had black name plates with white letters. One read 'employees only'.

One read 'Men', while the one on the opposite side read 'Women'. Another one said 'Security', and the last two doors both had plates that read 'Supplies'.

"Now what?" Conner whispered as we padded silently down the hall.

"I don't know," I answered, my mind spinning. I knew nothing about water towers and facilities. This was all stuff that I had no clue about. And I had no idea how we would stop the water from flowing into the city . . . if it already wasn't too late.

"We need to find the main power switches," Conner suggested. "That way, maybe we can just shut off the power to the whole plant. Nothing will work if there isn't any electricity."

That seemed like the best idea. In our house, we have a panel in the wall that has electrical shut-offs. Dad says it's dangerous, and that if I ever go near it, I'll be grounded.

But here, at the water plant, more was at stake. If we didn't stop the water from reaching the city, that would mean it would begin flowing into homes. If it flowed into homes, then people would drink it. If they drank it . . . .

I shuddered. *Don't think about it, Leah,* I told myself. *Don't think about it. Just concentrate on shutting down the water plant.*

At the end of the hall was a large, framed photograph. It was a picture of the new building and the water tower, taken from an airplane or a helicopter. I could see my reflection in the glass, and Conner's shadow, too.

But, to my horror, I could also see the reflection of two long claws behind us, reaching out from a door that had just swung open!

I spun and tried to run, but it was too late. The claw grasped my shoulder, so tightly that there was no way I could wriggle free!

22

Horror . . . then relief. I was horrified at first, because I was sure the dark reflection in the picture showed spider claws behind us, reaching out to snare Conner and I.

I was relieved to find that it was only a man! Whew!

He was wearing a dark blue uniform, and a blue hat. He looked like he might have been a police officer. The plate on the open door and an embroidered patch on the man's shirt both read

'Security'.

"And just what are we up to, hmmmm?" he snarled. Both of his hands had a death-grip on our shoulders. He wasn't going to let us go anywhere.

Neither Conner nor I said a word. I was still trying to catch my breath! He'd really frightened me.

"What's going on here?" he demanded again. I could tell he was already losing patience with us.

"Uh, um," I stammered. My tongue was tied up in knots, and I didn't know what to say. Down the hallway, behind the security guard, my eyes caught sight of the restroom signs.

Bingo.

"Just . . . just looking for the bathrooms," I blurted out, pointing down the hall.

The security guard looked over my shoulder at the restroom signs, then glared suspiciously back at us.

"They're right there," he stated flatly, motioning with a slight cock of his head. "You were going the other way. Why?" His beady, bulging eyes leered at us.

I didn't have an answer. At least, nothing was coming to me. Or Conner, for that matter. We both stood still, unable to move, locked in the clutches of the burly security officer.

"This is a private building," he huffed menacingly, "and you two are trespassing. Come with me."

As if we had a choice! He had such a tight grip on my shoulder that I thought he was going to break it.

He paraded Conner and I down a brightly lit hallway until we came to an open door. He marched us inside a small room. There were four chairs and a table, nothing else.

"You wait right here," he ordered, turning to leave.

"But . . . but you don't understand," Conner pleaded. "It's not what you think. It's really not!"

"I understand just perfectly," the officer answered harshly. He frowned, and his eyebrows scrunched together. "You two are up to no good. Wait here."

He closed the door, and I heard keys jingling. A lock clunked. The security officer's footsteps plodded down the hall until we could no longer hear them.

I tried the doorknob, but it wouldn't turn. I looked around for someplace where we might be able to slip out.

Nothing.

We were trapped. We were locked in a small room with no windows, and no hope of escape.

There's an expression used in boxing when a boxer can't fight any more, and the manager calls off the bout. It's called 'throwing in the towel'. When there is no hope in sight, the manager will end the contest by tossing in a white towel or kerchief into the ring.

That's how I felt. We'd come so far, only to fail. There was no hope now. Soon, the water would begin to flow, and there was nothing we — or anyone — could do. We'd done the best we could, but it just wasn't good enough.

Not good enough.

We were too late. Conner and I had failed to stop the Octogres from implementing their devious plan.

We had failed in our attempt to stop the evil octogores. It was time for Conner and I to give up, and throw in the towel.

23

I slumped down into a cold, white chair. Conner did the same. Neither of us spoke. Outside the door, I knew that time was racing by, but inside the cold confines of our white-walled prison, we knew there was nothing we could do.

So close, I thought, overcome with fear and frustration. *We'd come so close, only to fail miserably.* I knew Conner felt the same way. It showed on his face and in his eyes. He, too, knew that we were beyond hope. The only thing we could do was sit and wait.

We were both wallowing so much in our own self-pity that neither of us saw the tiny creature crawl beneath the door—until it began to grow!

The movement caught me by surprise and I leapt out of my chair and backed up to the far wall. I still wasn't used to seeing tiny spiders grow and change into humans, and I probably never would. Conner stood up and backed against the wall, too.

Who was it? Was it Mr. Emerson? Perhaps another arachno-sapien that we hadn't met yet?

Legs squirmed and contorted, and, as the spider grew, he became more and more human-like. More and more like—

Jarred Rook!

"Hey guys!" he exclaimed under his breath. I was about to speak, but he placed a finger to his lips. *"I saw that guy catch you,"* he said. *"Hang on a second, and I'll get you out of here!"*

Once again, he began to shrink and change back to a spider. In seconds, he was just a tiny creature. He slipped beneath the door and was gone.

We waited a moment, until the door suddenly chugged open. Jarred, now looking more like a human, stood holding the knob, nervously glancing up and down the hall.

"Hurry!" he whispered. "We don't have much time!"

We sprang from the small room and sprinted down the hall, following Jarred.

"There's a master control room on the second floor!" he exclaimed. "The water isn't flowing yet, but it will at any minute. The men at the controls are humans . . . they have no idea what the octogores are about to do!"

We had to stop them. I didn't know how, but we had to try. Even if we could just make them wait a few minutes before the water valves opened, then maybe we could avert disaster.

"This way!" Jarred said, and we followed him through a door and up a flight of stairs. Another door led to more stairs, and we raced up them.

We'd made it to the second floor!

At the other end of the hall was a series of windows. We could look through the windows and see all kinds of controls, blinking lights. Lots of meters, switches, and dials. Whoever was in charge of running this equipment really had to know what they were doing!

But then I saw something else, and my heart

sank like a lead balloon.

A cocoon! And another one!

"What . . . what are those??!" I stammered.

Jarred looked where I was pointing. "Uh-oh," he said.

The three of us looked through the window, and our worst fears were confirmed.

Two octogores had captured the human workers! They had captured the human workers and wrapped them up into cocoons!

And what's more . . . *the octogores were at the controls!* Their huge, hulking bodies seemed to fill the whole room, and their tree-like legs reached out in all directions.

This was far worse than I had imagined. I hadn't thought that the octogores would actually take control of the water plant. Yet here they were, in front at the controls, about to commit an unspeakable act. They were about to open the release valve . . . and begin letting the poison flow into the city!

24

One of the octogores raised a huge, gnarled claw, and began opening a valve.

"No!" Jarred shouted, running through the door into the control room. "No! Stop!" Even as he spoke, he began to change back into a spider, preparing for battle. Within seconds, Jarred's body had been transformed from a human to a spider!

The other octogore turned and faced Jarred, and attacked.

But the valve was almost open! There was no

way that Jarred would have time to fight the spider and then stop the other octogore! The water would begin flowing in seconds!

My brain raced, and my eyes scanned the control room. *What could I do?!?! How could I stop him?!?!*

The answer, of course, was that I couldn't. I couldn't, unless —

My eyes frantically scanned the control room. *There!*

On the other side of the room was a long, red lever. A black plate with white letters said:

EMERGENCY SHUT DOWN

I didn't waste another second. I shot by Conner and flew into the control room. Not four feet away, Jarred was battling the enormous octogore, but I didn't even think about it. I had only one thing on my mind: get to that lever. Get to that lever in time to stop the water from leaving the water plant. It was our last hope.

"Leah!" Conner shouted frantically. "Look out! One of them is coming for you!"

I raced even faster, more determined than ever

to reach the emergency shut off lever. Behind me, I could hear Jarred and the octogore fighting it out, crashing into equipment. Legs were flying, knocking over tables and chairs.

Almost there. Just a few more steps. *Just a few more —*

A sticky, stringy substance hit my shoulder, snapping me around. I pulled away, but was instantly struck with another web around my waist. I resisted the urge to grab it, knowing that my hands would be stuck to it if I did. Instead, I leapt forward, arms outstretched, reaching for the lever, reaching —

Got it!

I held the lever in both hands and began to pull. Another sticky string hit me, this time wrapping around my shoulder. I was being pulled away, but I held onto the handle with all my might. The octogore was still at the controls on the other side of the room, but he was trying to pull me away from the emergency shut off lever.

Boy, was I about to show him a trick!

I held the lever tightly, refusing to let go, even though the octogore was threatening to pull me away. However, the more the giant spider tugged, the tighter I gripped the lever — *until it swung sideways, shutting off the water release!* The octogore had actually pulled me hard enough to shut off the valve!

I allowed myself to feel a small bit of satisfaction, knowing that I'd stopped the water from flowing . . . at least for the time being.

I let go of the lever and the octogore began reeling in the webbing, pulling me across the floor. I struggled, but it was useless. There was no way I was going to escape.

Jarred and the other octogore were still fighting, and I looked up through the window.

Mr. Emerson! He made it, after all! Hooray!

He charged into the room with a large, silver cannister in his hand. It looked like a can of spray paint, only it was a little bit bigger. He raised the can and pointed it at the octogore . . . just as the octogore grabbed me with one of his legs!

Mr. Emerson lowered the can. "I can't use it!" he cried out. "The acid-ice might get you, as well!"

This was just not my day.

The huge octogore swung me up in the air, and I was afraid that he was going to let go and send me crashing to the floor. Instead, he began wrapping me up in webbing!

I screamed, struggling to keep the web from

wrapping around me, but it was no use. I spun around and around, helpless.

While I was spiraling in the firm clutches of the octogore, I caught a quick, blurry glimpse at Mr. Emerson, and he was quickly morhping into a spider.

"Hurry, Mr. Emerson!" I panicked. *"Hurry!!"*

A string of web caught me in the face and I tried to wipe it away.

Then, the octogore *did* drop me! He let me go, and I tumbled to the floor in a heap. The force knocked the wind from me as I hit the floor, and I immediately began to pull at the webbing around my legs and waist. Ugh! This stuff was gross.

Mr. Emerson had finished morphing into a spider, and he began fighting the octogore! As I looked around the room, it looked like some bizarre science fiction movie had come to life. Four huge spiders were fighting in the control room: Jarred, Mr. Emerson, and the two octogores!

But where had Conner gone? And where was Angela? Had Angela returned with Mr. Emerson?

Some of the web was still stuck to me, but I was finally able to pull it away and get up.

I sprinted, crossing the floor of the master control room to the door. On the floor was the can of acid-ice that Mr. Emerson had brought from the safe in the school laboratory. I snatched it up, and ran down the hall.

"Conner!" I yelled, my voice echoing down the corridor. *"Angela!"*

I came to a window, stopped, and looked down. Outside, the crowd of people stilled milled about below, filling the parking lot and the adjacent lawn. While I watched, a man in a fancy, dark suit pulled out a very large pair of scissors. He held them in the air for a moment, then reached down and cut a blue ribbon that had been placed across the front steps of the new building. Everyone clapped and cheered. No one in the crowd seemed aware of what was taking place in the water plant at that very moment.

Suddenly, a piercing scream echoed down the hall!

I bolted like lightning, because there was no mistaking that scream.

That scream was Angela!

I darted around a corner, following Angela's frantic pleading.

"I'm coming, Angela!" I cried. "Hang on! I'm coming!"

Rounding another hall, I suddenly froze, gasping in horror.

Conner was nowhere to be found—and an octogore had Angela in its clutches! On the ground was a can of Mr. Emerson's acid-ice! It must have been knocked out of Angela's hands!

But this octogore wasn't going to mess around. No more spinning webs or cocoons. It held Angela tightly with two legs, just inches from its two, dagger-like teeth. Its mouth opened, and Angela screamed like I had never heard her scream before in her life.

Angela was going to be eaten alive!

25

I raced to her rescue.

At least, I *hoped* I was racing to her rescue. I had never used Mr. Emerson's acid-ice before, and I really didn't know *how* to use it.

And that was another problem. What would happen if I used it on the giant spider while it was holding Angela? Would she turn to ice, too? After all, Mr. Emerson had been afraid to use the acid-ice on the octogore while it was holding me.

But there was no more time to think about it.

If I didn't act quickly, Angela would be a goner.

I ran up as close as I dared to the creature, and sprayed a little bit of the acid-ice on its leg. The can hissed, and a white mist streamed out.

The effect was immediate. The spider let out a chilling, piercing squeal, instantly dropping Angela. She fell to the floor and began crawling away.

The area where I'd sprayed the acid-ice began to turn blue! The spider was screeching and making weird noises. As soon as Angela had scrambled away, I let loose with another blast, this time aiming right for the body of the spider.

Suddenly, the spider stop screeching. Its entire body . . . legs, head and all . . . turned blue—*and froze!* It was unbelievable! The creature simply froze right where it was standing. The acid-ice went to work, swiftly racing over all parts of the spider! In seconds, it began to crumble before our very eyes! The huge beast seemed to struggle, then fell, its legs unable to support its body. Its body began to crumble and fall apart. Soon, it was just as Mr. Emerson said: the creature was reduced to nothing more than a powdery dust that covered the floor!

Angela looked dazed, and her eyes were watery. "You saved my life," she said. "You saved my life."

"What are friends for?" I replied, walking toward her. I helped her to her feet. "Just call me Leah, Queen Octogore Killer," I grinned smartly.

"Whatever," Angela answered. "But thanks for saving me. Thanks for—"

"Oh my gosh!" I interrupted. My jaw fell in horror. "Jarred! And Mr. Emerson! They're fighting off the octogores in the control room! We've got to help them!"

Angela snapped up her can of acid-ice, and we ran from the room . . . but we didn't get far. Not one, but two octogores were blocking our way!

And what was worse, the two octogores had been waiting for us. They knew we were coming!

And the first thing they did was use their powerful legs to knock the cans of acid-ice out of our hands. The canister went flying, bouncing to the floor, and out of our reach.

And, before we could do anything, the enormous octogores attacked.

26

There were two octogores . . . one on either side of us in the hall, and they both rushed at the same time.

"Back into the room!" I shouted, and we quickly dashed back and slammed the door. I could hear the spiders outside trying to get in, but Angela bolted the door just in time.

We were safe — at least for the time being.

However, we were kind of stuck, and we didn't have the cans of acid-ice . . . but at least we were safe — away from the octogores. Now what would we do?

On the other side of the room was a window, and I hurried over to it.

Below, in the parking lot, the grand opening celebration was continuing. I wondered if anyone had any clue as to what was going on in the water plant. Probably not. They were too busy making speeches and talking about all of their hard work, and talking about what the new plant will mean to the city.

Yeah, I thought. *I know exactly what it means to the city. Especially if the octogores succeed!*

"Leah, look!" Angela suddenly said, pointing.

I turned. She was focusing on a large vent on the far wall, near the floor. It looked like it was some sort of heating or air conditioning duct. It was about three feet wide and three feet high.

I knew what Angela was getting at. If we pulled off the cover, we might be able to escape through the large vent!

Question was . . . where did the vent lead to? If it led to a vacant room or service area, that would be fine.

But what if it led to a room below the building . . . where the main pipes were? The place might be crawling with octogores!

Either way, it looked like it was going to be our only way out. Without the acid-ice, I was afraid to go anywhere in the building. And we could still hear the octogores outside the room, tearing at the door, trying to get at us. It wouldn't be long before they would succeed in ripping the door from its hinges.

The vent in the wall was the only way out.

"Let's do it!" I said, nodding.

We ran to the other side of the room. Angela used a pen to pry the vent screen from the wall. It fell to the floor with a loud *clang!*, exposing a gaping square hole.

I looked at Angela, and she looked at me.

"I'm older," I said bravely. "Me first."

She didn't argue. I think we were both afraid, but *someone* had to go first.

That someone was *me*.

And what we were about to find still haunts me to this very day.

27

I climbed into the square chute. The metal was cold and smooth.

"Hold my hand," I ordered Angela. "Hold my hand so that we don't—"

At that very second, I lost my footing in the shaft, and began to slide down the cold, metal chute.

"*Leah!*" Angela screamed. "*Leah! Hang on! Hang on tight!!*"

But I lost my grip on her wrist. In a split-second, she disappeared from my view. I was sliding down the vent, picking up speed with every passing moment.

Flying down the vent wasn't the scary part. The scary part was wondering just where I would end up.

I could hear Angela's frantic shouts fade away, and soon, all I could hear was the swishing of my clothing against the metal chute. My body twisted and turned with the bends of the small tunnel, faster and faster as I slid deeper and deeper. I couldn't see a thing, and my fear swelled with every second. I couldn't help but think that, at the bottom of the chute, an enormous octogore waited for me, mouth open wide, teeth flared, ready to gobble me up. It wasn't a pleasant thought, and I pressed my hands against the sides of the metal to try and slow down, but it was no use.

Wherever I was going, I was on my way in a hurry!

After a couple more sharp twists and unexpected turns, I began to slow down. The chute seemed to be leveling out. Then I slid to a slow stop at the bottom of the vent.

I struggled out of the chute and found myself in a dark room. I was in complete darkness, and it freaked me out. I was afraid to even move, for fear of tripping over something and falling.

Then I heard a swishing sound in the chute, and I knew Angela was on her way. I could hear her as she twisted and turned down the square, metal tunnel. After a few seconds, I could hear her body slide to a stop.

"Leah?" she said nervously.

"Right here," I answered. I reached down in the darkness, found her feet, and helped her up.

"Where are we?" she asked.

"I don't really know," I replied. "Somewhere beneath the water plant, I guess."

"I hope there aren't any of those overgrown bugs around," Angela whispered.

"Spiders aren't bugs," I insisted. "Octogores aren't, either."

"Yeah, well, they're creepy, no matter what they are. Spiders, bugs, octogores, whatever. They're gross."

"Come on," I whispered, clasping her hand in the darkness. "We've got to find a way out of here. We have to find Conner. And Jarred, and Mr. Emerson."

I reached out with my free hand and felt a cold,

hard wall. We walked slowly in the darkness, wary of anything that we might stumble over or upon.

And then my hand felt a light switch. I clicked it on instantly, and a dim, yellow bulb breathed faint light from the ceiling above.

We were in some underground garage of sorts. There were no windows, but in the dull light of the yellow bulb I could see a few big trucks parked side by side, along with other pieces of heavy equipment.

But we also saw something else, causing both Angela and I to gasp in complete horror. We froze, our mouths hanging open, shocked at what we had discovered.

There was no doubt about it: what we were seeing was the most gruesome, unbelievable sight I had ever seen.

28

Cocoons.   There were dozens of them, wrapped tightly and hanging everywhere—the walls, the ceiling, the corners of the room.   Fuzzy, white cocoons were suspended from dark corners and shadowy crevices. Most of them were high up in the air above our heads. Each cocoon was about the size of a beach ball, only more oval-shaped.

Angela and I stared, our mouths frozen open.

"What . . . what are they?" she asked.

"I'm not sure," I replied quietly. "But I think

that they're eggs. I'll bet this is the place that Jarred Rook was talking about. I think this is where the octogores have laid their eggs."

It was a horrifying, awful thought. There were dozens of egg sacs affixed to the walls, to the ceiling—everywhere. I couldn't even imagine the fact that there were probably thousands—maybe even *millions*—of octogores in each tightly wound ball of webbing.

A cold snake slithered straight down my spine, and I shuddered. The room around us was strangely quiet, and the white egg sacs hanging from the walls and ceiling seemed motionless—but I knew better. I knew that inside each one of those egg sacs, thousands of baby octogores were growing, waiting to hatch.

Just the *thought* caused every hair on my body to stand straight up.

"Come on," I whispered to Angela. "Let's get out of here. This place is creeping me out."

"Yeah, me too," Angela replied, her head still tilted back, gazing up at the milky-white cocoons.

We tip-toed around a few of the vehicles. Our feet padded the floor as we walked, sneaking in and around the parked trucks.

"Leah!" Angela whispered, pointing. *"There's a garage door ahead!"*

She was right. On the other side of a row of utility trucks was a large garage door. It was closed, and had no windows. I was certain it would provide a way out.

We began walking faster, and my relief grew with every step. I wanted out of this place as fast as I could.

I managed a quick glance over my shoulder, taking another look at the octogore eggs suspended on the walls and ceiling. Mr. Emerson needed to know about this. He could take care of this problem, I was sure.

In the dim light, Angela and I walked around an idle crane that sat motionless near the garage door.

At least, I had *thought* it was a crane. Unfortunately for us, we were about to find that it wasn't a crane, after all.

29

We were almost to the garage door.

Home free, I thought. This insane nightmare would soon be over. Soon, I'd be home. Soon, I'd be safe. All we would have to do is open the door, and we'd be out.

It wasn't going to be that easy.

Without warning, the crane we were next to came to life!

Oh my gosh! my mind screamed. *It's not a crane! It's a SPIDER!! It's an OCTOGORE!*

It was bigger than any octogore I'd seen so far. Twenty feet tall, with legs that arched high into the air. In the faint, yellow light I could see its piercing, black eyes, leering at us.

And it began to move! Using its huge, thick legs, it raised its body high into the air.

"Angela!" I screamed. "Come on! Get under the truck!"

I grabbed Angela, and we both dove to the hard cement floor.

"Roll under the truck!" I shouted. "It's the only place where it might not be able to reach us!"

We scrambled beneath a parked truck. Behind me, I could see the octogore's strong legs reaching out, trying to grab hold of us. Once, it almost got my pant leg, but I pulled back just in time.

We kept crawling, fleeing from the attacking octogore. Its legs were long, and the creature was trying to reach under the truck and pull us out. And I'm sure the creature would have succeeded, too . . . if it weren't for a sudden shout we heard at the other end of the garage.

"Leah!?!? Angela!?!?" the loud voice echoed through the big room.

I'd know that voice anywhere!

"Conner!" I shouted. "We're over here! But watch out! We're being attacked!"

I could hear Conner's feet drumming across the cement floor. The octogore was still trying to catch us, but when Conner burst onto the scene, the creature was distracted. The disturbance gave Angela and I enough time to scramble out from the other side of the truck.

"Conner!" I shouted. My voice boomed around the large room. "You okay?!?!?"

"I ran out to Mr. Emerson's van to get more cans of acid-ice!" he hollered. "I've got—"

His voice stopped abruptly, and all we could hear were the rustling sounds of the enormous octogore as his legs swished against the concrete, searching for us. I decided to take a peek around the corner of the truck.

The giant spider was there, alright . . . *and so was Conner!* He looked like a tiny doll in front of the huge octogore! Conner was holding out a can of acid-ice, bravely pointing it up at the towering, black creature.

"Spray him!" I shouted. "Spray him with the acid-ice!"

"I'm trying!!" Conner insisted. *"But the nozzle*

is stuck! I'm pressing the button . . . but nothing is happening!"

Oh no!

"Run!" I shrieked. "Run! Get away from him!"

The huge beast was blocking our exit, and Conner would only be able to run the other way.

But it was already too late.

The creature suddenly surged forward with a burst of incredible power and speed. Its hungry mouth was open, exposing two sword-like fangs.

Without the acid-ice, Conner wasn't even going to have a chance.

30

Angela and I both screamed as the sinister beast attacked. Conner tried to jump back, but the spider knocked him to the ground. He rolled frantically on the concrete as the octogore tried to take a bite, narrowly missing with its two razor-sharp teeth.

The spider came down again. Conner was on his back, and when the creature opened his mouth to snare its prey, Conner did the only thing he could do: he drew his arm back—and hurled the can of acid-ice directly into the gaping mouth of the spider.

There was a split-second of hesitation as the spider drew closer to Conner. Then it chomped down violently on the can, closing its mouth, chewing.

Suddenly, it let out a thundering, terrible wail! The spider howled and screeched, so loud that I threw my hands over my ears. The noise was awful! I watched as the spider began to curl its legs in, then snap them back out again. It began to jerk and convulse.

Conner seized the opportunity to spring to his feet. He turned and ran to us, seeking cover behind the truck. The three of us watched as the giant spider jerked and twisted

Then, it stopped moving. It stood motionless for a moment, frozen in place. Its color began to change from a dark, rich black to an ice-cold blue. Within seconds, the creature seemed to be shaking on its feet, trembling. Legs gave way and snapped, and the hulking creature suddenly fell to the floor. In minutes, it was no more than a pile of dust.

"Okay," Angela whispered, after a long silence. "I vote that we never have to go through this again."

"Me too," I agreed. "Me too."

But we weren't in the clear yet. Just when we thought we'd be able to make it out of the garage safely, we heard another sound.

It was the sound of swishing legs, the sound of claws scraping on concrete. Then: a shadow! There was something coming toward us!

31

The dark form drew closer and closer.

Oh no! There were *two* of them! Two dark shadows were approaching quickly. They must have heard the commotion, and were coming to investigate!

We were about to run and try to get away when a voice called out.

"Leah? Is that you?"

It was Jarred Rook! Jarred and Mr. Emerson had found us!

It was the happiest—and luckiest—day of my life.

"We found the vent," Mr. Emerson explained as he and Jarred approached. "The cover was off, and we thought you had used the chutes to escape."

"That's exactly what we did," I answered.

"Were you able to stop the spiders?" Angela asked. "Is the water running to the city?"

"Yes, we were able to stop them," Jarred answered proudly. "And the water is running. Mr. Emerson was able to remove the barrel of poison before it was poured into the water. The workers are safe, and we used the acid-ice on the octogores."

I pointed to the ceiling behind Jarred and Mr. Emerson. "Look what we found!" I said excitedly.

Jarred and Mr. Emerson turned and spotted the egg sacs on the walls and ceiling.

"You found it!" Mr. Emerson exclaimed. "You found the octogore nest!"

"But what do we do with them?" Conner asked.

I was wondering the same thing myself.

"We do exactly what we did with the octogores," Jarred answered, gazing up at the cocoons suspended from the ceiling and walls.

Mr. Emerson nodded. "That's right," he agreed. "We'll spray the egg bundles with the acid-ice. That will take care of them for sure."

Mr. Emerson, Conner, and Jarred went to work spraying the fuzzy egg sacs. The white pouches turned a deep, ice-blue color before they crumbled into powder. The chalky dust disintegrated and fell to the floor, leaving a pile of fine, gray residue. In a few minutes, all of the eggs were destroyed.

"Well, now things can get back to normal," Mr. Emerson said.

"Normal?" I asked. "How? There's still octogores living in the tunnels beneath Saginaw!"

"Not for long," Mr. Emerson replied. "On our way back from the lab, I gave several other arachno-sapiens some cans of my acid-ice. They're in the pipes and tunnels this instant, taking care of the rest of the octogores. There is no way those evil creatures can win."

Still, I was wondering how things would ever get back to normal. Especially since I knew that there were arachno-sapiens living right here! Right here in Saginaw — my hometown!

What a freaky day this had turned out to be.

■■■

Conner, Angela and I walked home through the field. By now, the crowd in the parking lot had disappeared, and most people had gone home. There was a lot of talk at the water plant about giant spiders, mainly by the two control room engineers that had been wrapped up in webbing. No one believed them, and I think everyone in the plant cracked a lot of jokes . . . after all, if someone told me that they were kidnapped by a giant spider and wrapped up into a cocoon, I don't think I would have believed them, either!

But now, I knew better.

When we arrived home, I had another let-down. I was hoping that Grumpy would have returned — but there was no sign of him. I hadn't had much time to look for him today, but now I was *really* worried, and I feared the worst. He'd never been gone this long before, and I was sure that something awful had happened. I just couldn't bear the thought of Grumpy carried off by one of those ugly octogores.

Conner, Angela, and I sat in my house for a few minutes, trying to decide what to do. We'd searched all over, and still no luck. I guess I'd just wait until Mom and Dad came home. Then we could all go look for him again.

I said good-bye to Conner and Angela, and I sat down to do my homework. I hadn't been studying more than ten minutes when I suddenly heard a very familiar scraping on the door. My heart leapt, and I turned my head.

Grumpy! Grumpy was home! He had come back through the hole he'd dug under the fence in the back yard, and now he was at the sliding glass door, his wet nose pressed against the glass, wagging his tail happily.

My heart soared. "Grumpy!" I shouted, jumping up from my chair. But then, I froze.

Oh, it was good to see Grumpy, alright, and I sure was glad he was home . . . but it wasn't good to see what was behind him in the back yard.

A giant spider!

It was big and gross-looking, and it was coming toward the door!

It was coming for Grumpy!

32

I quickly slid the sliding glass door open and let Grumpy inside.

"C'mon, boy!" I urged. Grumpy's tail smacked the door happily as he bounded inside. I slammed the sliding glass door closed, horrified by the huge spider in the backyard. It was beginning to get dark, but I could see the spider, alright. Long, wiry legs moved slowly, one after the other. The spider was all black, with two eyes glaring menacingly at me.

But . . . just what was it? An Arachno-Sapien?

An octogore? I couldn't tell, and I wasn't going to take any chances.

I backed away from the door. Grumpy saw the spider coming toward the house, and he hardly paid attention! He acted like he didn't have a care in the world, and certainly wasn't concerned about any spider, no matter how big it was!

But the spider kept coming. It climbed up the back porch and came right up to the glass!

Suddenly, there was a scraping sound at the *front* door! I turned, and in the window—

Another spider!

But what was worse, the front door was opening! The spider was coming inside!!

Oh no! They were coming for me! *The octogores knew where I lived, and they were coming to get me!*

I gasped, and my hands flew to my mouth, muffling a scream. There was nowhere I could go, no place to run.

Then the sliding glass door behind me slid open! The spiders were ganging up on me!

Oh, how I wished I would have brought some of Mr. Emerson's acid-ice home with me! That would have taken care of them for sure!

But there was hope. I wasn't positive that they were octogores. They could be arachno-sapiens. They could be friends of Jarred or Mr. Emerson.

I crossed my fingers, hoping for the best. If these spiders were octogores, I was in a lot of trouble.

Suddenly, one of the spiders began to change!

Whew! They *were* only arachno-sapiens! I breathed easier, knowing that I'd soon find out who they really were.

And when the spiders slowly changed back into human form, and when I realized what, and who, they were, I just about passed out. Nothing ever could have prepared me for what I was about to see.

33

As the spiders morphed and began to change, I looked carefully for recognizable features. I was sure that they had to be friends from school or something. I was actually proud of myself for not panicking and getting all freaked out.

But there was something strange going on. Something really weird.

I was watching the spider by the front door, watching its face for features I might recognize.

Suddenly, I almost collapsed to the floor!

When the face began to take shape, I knew for sure that I was dreaming. That's all there was to it. I'd been dreaming, and I'd be waking up any second.

Because the face I was seeing was the face of— *Mom!*

It was impossible, but it was true! *The spider at the front door turned out to be my mom!*

Likewise, the spider behind me, in the kitchen by the sliding glass door, was my *dad!*

"Hello, Leah," Mom said gently. She had returned to human form now. This was bizarre!

"Hi, honey," Dad said, smiling.

"But . . . but . . . ." was all I could say.

"I know what you're thinking, and the answer is 'yes'," Mom said. She walked over to where I was standing. "We are arachno-sapiens. We couldn't tell you right away, though. We wanted to wait until you were older. We thought it would be better that way."

"You're . . . you're . . . *arachno-sapiens?!?!?*" I said, my mouth hanging open. I was dumbfounded. I still couldn't believe what I was hearing!

"Yes," Dad replied, nodding his head. "That's right. Which of course, means that *you—*"

I gulped.

"—you are an arachno-sapien, too," he

finished. "You, Leah, are part human, and part spider."

"But . . . but . . . ." I was still having a difficult time speaking. I grew light-headed, and my thoughts were reeling.

Me?!?!? An arachno-sapien?!?!? How could that be? I *hate* spiders! I don't like anything about them!

"And what. . . what about Scott?" I stammered. "Is Scott an arachno-sapien, too?"

"Of course," Dad answered. "Your brother is an arachno-sapien as well. He just doesn't know it yet. He will, though, very soon."

"In time," Mom said gently, "you'll appreciate what and who you are. We wanted to give you a chance to grow up normally, like other kids your age. We thought it would be easier for you this way."

"But . . . but the octogores," I exclaimed. "What about them?"

Dad reached out and put his hand on my shoulder. "They're all taken care of," he said. "That's where your mother and I have been today. We all had to band together to stop the octogores. As a matter of fact, I saw you today. I *helped* you today."

"Huh? You did? How? Where?!?"

"In the field, when you and Conner fell into the pit. I was in the drain pipe, watching for octogores. I was the one who helped you and Conner out of the hole."

"That was you?!?!?" I exclaimed. *"You're the spider that helped us?!?!?"*

Dad smiled. "That's where your mother and I have been all day," he explained. "When Mr. Emerson told us that the octogores had arrived, all of the arachno-sapiens pulled together to stop them. And you, sweetheart, helped us out a great deal. More than you'll ever know. I know you've never liked spiders, Leah, but I think you'll get used to it. I think you'll really like being an arachno-sapien."

His words hung in my head.

Me? Leah Warner? *An arachno-sapien?* Part spider, part human?

Crazy.

"Does . . . does that mean that I can . . . turn into a spider? Like you and Mom? And Jarred? And Mr. Emerson?"

Mom smiled. "That's right, Leah. You can turn into a spider, whenever you want to. Just like us. And your friend Jarred Rook. And Mr. Emerson. And a lot of other people that you know. There are a few hundred of us — arachno-sapiens, that is — that live here in Saginaw. We all can change into spiders. Would you like us to show you how?"

I had to really think about that. Spiders are gross. Or, at least, I thought they were.

But now, I was a spider! Part spider, anyway. I couldn't believe it. I couldn't believe it, but I guessed I'd better just get used to it.

"Would you like to learn?" Dad asked.

Slowly, I nodded my head. "Okay," I squeaked shyly. "I'm kind of scared, though."

Mom squeezed my hand. "There's nothing to be afraid of," she assured. "You'll be fine. It'll take a while to get the hang of it, but you'll do great. Ready?"

Again, I nodded. I wasn't really ready, but I figured that if I was an arachno-sapien, I'd better figure out just what it all meant.

Dad grasped one hand, and Mom held the other.

"Close your eyes," Dad said. "Close your eyes, and begin to see what a spider sees. Begin to think like a spider. Begin to think that you have eight legs, and can climb up walls. Think like a spider, Leah . . . think. Think like a spider."

I tried. I really did. My eyes were closed tightly, and I tried to pretend that I was looking around and seeing my eight legs, seeing my web where I lived, stuff like that. I felt kind of stupid, but I did what Dad said.

"*Okay,*" I heard Mom say. "*Open you eyes, Leah. Go ahead and open your eyes . . . .*"

34

I opened my eyes.

Yikes! I had eight legs! My skin had become a hard, brown shell. I'm a spider! I'm an arachnosapien!

Mom and Dad had changed back into spiders, too, and they were still standing next to me.

"See?" Mom said encouragingly—but her mouth never moved! I could hear her voice, but my mom—that spider—didn't seem to be actually *speaking!* It was as if she were communicating through brain waves!

"You're okay," she communicated. " You'll do fine."

"Are . . . are you really *talking?*" I asked, but then I realized that I didn't really 'speak' either! My 'spider' mouth never moved!

"It's how we communicate when we change into spiders," Dad answered. "We don't speak. All you have to do is *think* what you want to say. I think you're going to like being an arachno-sapien."

And do you know what? Dad was right! I really think I could get used to having eight legs and being able to climb up and down trees and walls really easy!

I tried walking, but it was really clumsy. I banged into a chair, and then I bumped the wall. Don't laugh! I'd like to see *you* try and walk with six more legs! It's not very easy.

"It'll get easier the more you walk," Dad reassured me. "It'll be awkward the first few times, but soon, you'll find that eight legs can really be useful."

Dad was right. The more I tried moving about in the living room, the better I became at using my eight legs. Sure, it would take a while to get used to, but I was getting the hang of it. Being an arachno-sapien was going to be fun!

"I can't wait to tell everyone!" I exclaimed.

Dad shook his head. "No," he said. "That isn't a good idea. It's best that you keep your secret to yourself. Like the rest of us. That way, we can all live here in peace. We all live here in Saginaw, and soon, you'll meet many more people who are just like you. But you must keep it a secret among us. No one can know. Do you understand?"

"Yes," I said. "I guess so."

Drats. I thought it would be kind of cool to go to school and show everyone how I could turn into a spider! There's a kid in my class who's always bugging me, and I would *love* to give him the shock of his life!

"Do you promise to keep our secret?" Mom asked.

I nodded. "I promise," I replied, looking down at my strange body.

Wow . . . it's funny how your life can change in one single day.

35

As the weeks passed, I spent more and more time as a spider. Dad and Mom showed me how to shrink and become smaller. And they showed me how to climb and spin webs and all kinds of things. I met a lot of new friends that were arachno-sapiens, too. Even the basketball coach at school was an arachno-sapien! They had been all around me . . . in school, on the next block—all over the place, and no one knew it! Being an arachno-sapien wasn't bad, after all. I really began to enjoy changing into a spider and changing back into a human.

A couple weeks after school was dismissed for the summer, Mom, Dad, Scott and I went on vacation. We always go to neat places, and this time we went to a tiny town up north called Great Bear Heart. That's right—Great Bear Heart. It's a small village on Puckett Lake, and it's beautiful! The air is fresh and sweet, and there are lots of trees and beaches. We stayed at a place near the lake called *Lazy Shores Resort.*

And that's where I found the huge footprints in the mud.

I was down by the lake, swimming. Grumpy was there, too, and I was throwing a stick into the water for him to retrieve. Once, Grumpy didn't bring the stick back to me. He took it into the woods and disappeared.

"Grumpy!" I shouted, clapping my hands. "Come on, boy!"

When he didn't return, I walked into the woods to get him. I found him sniffing the ground near an old stump.

But that wasn't all I found.

Footprints— *enormous footprints*— were sunk into the soft ground around the stump!

I knelt down to get a closer look. The prints were HUGE! Whoever—or whatever—made these footprints, had to be ten feet tall!

And it was then that I heard the crunching of brush and snapping of twigs.

Someone—or something—was coming!

36

I turned suddenly, and was about to morph into a spider. I'd gotten pretty good at it by now, and I knew that if some big, hairy creature saw a gigantic spider, it might think twice about trying to gobble me up!

But there was no monster attacking. It was just a boy! A boy about my age, holding a mayonnaise jar, walking toward me. He was wearing a knapsack on his back, and a baseball cap on his head.

"Hi," he said, waving with his free hand.

"Hello," I replied, relieved.

Grumpy quit sniffing the ground, snapped up his stick, and ran up to him. The boy stopped walking and bent down to pet Grumpy. He took the stick from him and threw it into the lake. Grumpy bounded through the brush, across the sandy beach, and leapt into the water.

"Cool dog," the boy said.

"That's Grumpy," I replied. "He *loves* the water. And sticks."

The boy took a few steps closer. He was carrying the jar carefully, like he was afraid of breaking something.

"I'm Leah," I offered.

"Parker," he introduced. "Parker Smith."

"What have you got in the jar?" I asked curiously.

"Well, I'll show you, but I'm not sure if you're going to like it."

He held out the jar. Inside was a spider that was about the size of a baseball!

"I found him up by my house," he explained. "Mom wanted to kill him, but I didn't want her to. I caught it and brought him down here to let him go in the woods. I think spiders are cool, but, being a girl, you probably don't like them much."

"Oh," I said, smiling, "I think spiders are okay. In fact, I think they're pretty cool."

And with that, I took the jar from him, opened the lid . . . and poured the spider into my hand!

"Spiders are my friends," I said smartly.

Parker just about fell over! He couldn't believe what I was doing!

"What . . . but . . . how . . . ?" He wasn't sure what to say. He'd probably never seen a girl holding a real, live, wild spider in her hand before.

If only I could tell him who I really was!

"Hey!" he exclaimed. "That's awesome! I mean, even I'm not brave enough to do that!"

"Oh, spiders don't bother anyone," I said smiling. "As long as they're left alone."

I lowered the creature to the ground, and it quickly scrambled off into the grass.

Parker and I talked for a little while. He was pretty cool. Up until then, I hadn't met anyone my age in the tiny town of Great Bear Heart. It was kind of fun to meet someone that was my age.

"What do you do for fun around here?" I asked him. "It seems like a pretty small town."

"Oh, it used to be really boring," Parker

answered. "Until last summer. Until we formed the Adventure Club. Then all kinds of crazy things happened."

"The *what?*" I asked.

"The Adventure Club," he replied, nodding his head. "There are six of us. We were bored out of our skulls, so we formed a group, and we call it the Adventure Club. We even have our own clubhouse on the other side of the town, high in an old maple tree. We have a great time." He threw his thumb over his shoulder, motioning toward the small town.

"Like, what do you do?" I quizzed. "Have adventures? Stuff like that?"

Parker Smith nodded his head. "You wouldn't believe the things we do," he replied, shaking his head. "We have a lot of fun. Sometimes we get into trouble, like the time we found the old cemetery. That was pretty spooky."

"But what about these?" I asked, pointing to the huge footprints on the ground.

"Oh," Parker said, smirking. "Bigfoot. Yeah, I know all about that. That's another crazy story in itself."

I looked down at the tracks, then back up at Parker.

"Bigfoot?!?!" I exclaimed. "You've got to tell me," I begged.

"Okay," Parker agreed. "I'll start right from the beginning . . . ."

Bigfoot Runs Amok

(a complete story from the book 'GHOST IN THE
GRAVEYARD' by Johnathan Rand!)

1

We didn't mean to send the town of Great Bear Heart
into complete panic, but that's just what happened
when the big footprints were discovered in the park
on the shores of Puckett Lake one summer day.

Of course, we were partially to blame, if not
mostly, since we were the ones who put the huge
tracks there in the first place.

It was just supposed to be a prank. We were
just trying to get back at Norm Beeblemeyer, the
reporter for the *Great Bear Heart Times*. Not a single
one of us thought that it would turn into the chaotic

situation it became.

The idea began with the president of the Adventure Club, Shane Mitchell. He had just called the meeting to order in our clubhouse, which sits high in an old maple tree on the other side of McArdle's farm. We used to get together in Shane's dad's garage, but after we had the fire, his father wouldn't allow us to meet there anymore. Not that we could have, anyway: the fire took out most of the garage, and almost burned down Shane's house. In the end, everything turned out for the better, anyway. The six of us in the club—Shane Mitchell, Holly O'Mara, Tony Gritter, Lyle Haywood, Dylan Bunker, and myself, Parker Smith—spent a whole week building the new clubhouse high in the branches of an enormous old tree. Even old Ralph McArdle couldn't see it, and it was on his property. The fort is almost completely hidden within the thick leaves, and from the other side of the field, you can't see it at all.

Which is a good thing, because we needed someplace that was secret. We couldn't let just *anybody* know what we were up to.

We had formed the Adventure Club out of pure desperation. Great Bear Heart, the small town where we all live, really doesn't have a lot to do. It's a great little town in Michigan on the shores of Puckett Lake, and while there's a lot of outdoorsy-type things to do like fishing, hunting, hiking and biking, that's about it. No skateboard parks, no bowling alley, and the closest movie theater is fifteen miles away in another town. The six of us had started the Adventure Club in an effort to have a little fun, and make things a bit more exciting.

And I must say this: I think we almost always succeed — because whenever we get mixed up into something, you can bet that normal everyday boredom goes right out the window.

"All right," Shane Mitchell said, holding up one hand and calling the meeting to order. He was sitting on an old blue plastic milk crate, one hand on his knees. Shane is thirteen, and the oldest member of the Adventure Club. "Wednesday's meeting of the Adventure Club is now in session. Do we have any business from last week's meeting that we need to discuss?" He looked around the room for volunteers.

Dylan Bunker hesitantly raised his chubby hand, cocking his head from side to side to see if anyone else had anything to say. Dylan is ten, and is the youngest in our group. He's got a mop of thick, fire-engine red hair that hangs over his forehead and nearly covers his eyes. Dozens of freckles dot his cheeks.

"I do," he squeaked. "I still haven't been paid back that four dollars and thirty-four cents that I loaned the club last month."

Tony Gritter let out a tired groan. Tony is twelve, and has short, wiry, blonde hair. "For crying out loud," he grumbled, shaking his head as he glared at Dylan. "The club owes all of us money. You bring this up every week. You'll get your money when we have it."

After the fire, it had taken all of the club's money to build the new clubhouse. We even had to dip into our own savings and contribute a few extra bucks to buy lumber and other materials.

"Give it a rest, Dylan," Holly O'Mara said, pulling a lock of her brown hair away from her eyes. "We'll all get our money back soon enough."

The matter was dropped. It had been agreed last month that as soon as the club came into some money, it would pay each of us back, plus a little bit of interest, if it could be afforded. Dylan Bunker looked a little disappointed. He didn't have a lot of money — but then again, none of us did. Dylan had been hoping to get paid back by now. I guess I couldn't blame him.

On this particular day, we were all still a bit miffed at Norm Beeblemeyer, the local reporter for the town's small newspaper, the *Great Bear Heart Times*. It's a weekly paper, and Norm is the only full-time reporter. He's kind of a dufus, and no one in the club likes him much, ever since he accused Tony Gritter of waxing the windows at the community library a few weeks ago. Sure, Tony is a prankster, but he'd never do anything that would cause any damage. Norm Beeblemeyer was proven wrong, of course, but not until Tony had already been blamed and even questioned by the police. To this day, Norm still believes that all of us in the Adventure Club had something to do with the vandalism at the library — and to this day, he is wrong about it.

There are a few more reasons why we don't like Norm Beeblemeyer, too. Since there's not much excitement in or around Great Bear Heart, there isn't a lot of news to report. To dig up a story, Norm Beeblemeyer sticks his nose into everybody's business, and most of what he reports in the paper just isn't true. There are more than a few people in Great Bear Heart, including all six of us in the Adventure Club, that would like to see Norm

Beeblemeyer get what's coming to him.

So, when the window-waxing incident blew over, our club voted 6-0 to somehow, some way, get back at Norm.

Which is how this whole Bigfoot thing came about.

2

The topic of discussion at our meeting had shifted from money matters to Norm Beeblemeyer, and what a creep he was. We all had devised plans to get even with him, but most of our ideas were either too far-fetched or just not practical.

"I know!" Dylan Bunker said excitedly. "Let's gather up a bunch of dog mess and wrap it up in newspapers! We'll light it on fire, set it on his front porch, and then we'll—"

"Ring the doorbell and run," Tony Gritter

finished snidely, taking the wind out of Dylan's sails. He continued, tiredly explaining Dylan's idea. "Norm opens the door, stomps on the fire to put it out, and gets dog mess all over his shoes." He shook his head. "That's the oldest trick in the book. Problem is, it doesn't work, and it'll probably catch his house on fire."

Dylan Bunker pursed his lips tightly, then, just as he was about to say something, Holly O'Mara spoke up, her eyes narrowed and her jaw tense. Like Lyle and Tony, Holly is twelve, but she looks older.

"We need to do something that proves to everyone that Norm Beeblemeyer is the creep he really is," she boiled.

We went around the room, bouncing ideas around. Finally, Shane Mitchell smiled, and one side of his lip curled up, then the other. Real slow-like, like he had an idea that was growing by the second. When he grinned like that, we knew he had a winner. And usually, when Shane Mitchell had an idea, you could bet it was a pretty good one.

Shane explained that he'd been reading a lot about 'Bigfoot' sightings out west . . . mostly in Montana, Idaho and Oregon. Bigfoot was supposed to be this huge, hairy creature that roamed the forests and mountains. He said the library has a couple of books that even have pictures of the beast.

"Awww, come on Shane," Lyle Haywood sneered. "Do you really believe all of that bunk?" He adjusted his glasses, then scratched his chin. Lyle is tall . . . tall and lanky. Skinny as a rail. He's the same age as Holly O'Mara, but man . . . Lyle Haywood should be in college, not in grade school. He's brilliant. He's also the skeptical one of the group. Lyle Haywood isn't likely to believe anything unless you can show it to him.

Shane Mitchell skewered his face into a sarcastic frown. "Of course I don't believe it," he insisted sharply, furrowing his brow. A wide, toothy smile returned to his face. "But what if, all of a sudden, there was a Bigfoot creature that roamed Puckett Lake?" His smile grew. "I bet we can make people believe it—*especially* a particular reporter from the local paper."

Hot diggity-dogs. I knew exactly what Shane was thinking.

Lyle Haywood grinned broadly, and so did I, then Holly O'Mara. Dylan Bunker hadn't yet figured out what Shane was talking about, and he had a questioning look on his face. Tony Gritter knew what

189

Shane was thinking, because a smile began to form on his lips, too, and soon it was an all-out smug grin.

And that's how the whole mess got started.

3

At the next club meeting, we arrived to find a brown burlap bag on the floor with a piece of paper on it. The paper read:

WARNING! BIGFOOTS INSIDE!

DON'T OPEN TILL I GET BACK!

"He spelled it wrong," Holly O'Mara pointed

out. 'Bigfoots' shouldn't be plural." Holly was meticulous when it came to grammar and spelling, and her school grades showed it.

"How do you put a Bigfoot in a bag?" Dylan Bunker wondered aloud. He poked at the burlap with a pudgy finger.

"Maybe it's one of those 'just add water' deals," Lyle Haywood smirked.

"Yeah," I said, chuckling. "Maybe they supersized a 'Smallfoot' for another thirty cents."

Just then, Shane Mitchell's head popped up through the trap door of the clubhouse. Our fort is thirty feet off the ground, and you have to climb up a long rope ladder to get inside. Once we're all here, we can pull the ladder up to keep everyone else out, should anyone happen to come upon our secret clubhouse on the edge of the field.

"Whaddya think?" Shane said, grinning as he closed the trap door beneath him.

"How can we know what to think?" Holly replied, shrugging her shoulders. "We don't even know what's in the bag."

"I'll bet it's one of those 'just add water' Bigfoots, isn't it, Shane?" Lyle offered with a toothy grin. Holly glared scornfully at him.

"Better," Shane Mitchell answered, and he wasted no time in opening up the burlap bag on the table. He pulled out two items and held them up.

Big feet. That's what they were—and I mean BIG feet! It was a pair of feet, carved carefully out of wood, complete with toes and everything. Great detail had gone into the underside of the foot, and it was complete with an arch and everything. The top of the feet were flat, and had two leather straps. They looked like big wooden snowshoes.

"What in the world are those?" Dylan Bunker asked.

"It's Bigfoot," Shane answered, clearly proud of himself. "I carved them out of some scrap lumber I found." He put the feet on the ground and demonstrated how they would work.

"See? You put your feet here like this," he explained, bending over and reaching for his feet, "then you buckle these two straps around your shoes like this. That's all there is to it."

The huge feet were secured tightly to his shoes, and Shane began to walk, taking giant strides. He looked like he had two big skateboards strapped to his feet—minus the wheels, of course. "All we have to do is take these out to the park and walk around in some of the real mushy parts," he continued. "I've already tried them by my house. They work great, and leave gigantic footprints on the ground!"

"That's cool!" Dylan Bunker exclaimed.

Lyle Haywood had a sneaky grin on his face, and Tony Gritter watched, his arms crossed. Holly O'Mara leaned forward on her milk crate, watching Shane suspiciously.

Shane clomped awkwardly around the wood floor of our clubhouse. He looked a bit silly as he plodded over the oak planks, but it was easy to see how his plan might work.

Tony Gritter was unconvinced. "So, we make big tracks in the swamp," he stated as Shane came to a stop in the middle of the room. "Then what?"

"Then we write a letter to the paper," Holly O'Mara proclaimed.

Shane snapped his fingers, pointed at Holly, and nodded his head excitedly. "That's exactly it!" he agreed, smiling at Holly and then at the rest of us around the room. "We write an anonymous letter to the paper, and tell them that some strange, ape-like creature has been spotted in the park near Puckett Lake. Of course, Norm Beeblemeyer will be the one to go investigate."

"When he does, he'll find the Bigfoot tracks!" Lyle Haywood interjected, slapping his hands together.

"He'll think it's a real creature!" I exclaimed.

Our faces lit up. It would be a great prank to pull on Norm Beeblemeyer, but, more importantly, it would feel good to get him back for being such a jerk to Tony Gritter.

Of course, we didn't think about what we would do *after* Norm Beeblemeyer went to investigate . . . but one thing was for certain: we didn't expect things to get out of hand the way they did.

4

The *Great Bear Heart Times* is published once a week, and delivered on Friday. Which means that we'd have to give Norm Beeblemeyer a couple days head-start if we wanted him to investigate the Bigfoot tracks in the park, and have something appear in Friday's paper. We all met at the clubhouse on Monday morning and carefully crafted a note. On a plain piece of paper, Holly O'Mara wrote:

To whom it may concern:

I know this might sound crazy, but yesterday, on my morning walk, I saw a very strange sight. It was a large creature that looked like an ape. It stood about eight feet tall and had hair all over its body. My, was I frightened! I rushed to tell my husband, but by the time we returned, the creature had disappeared into the forest. My husband wandered about a bit, and says that there are large footprints all over the place. I just thought someone should know. I'm not going to leave my name, because I know that you'll probably think my husband and I are both crazy. But there's something out there, I tell you. There's something in the forest, and I'm terrified. Someone should do something.

Signed,

Frightened in Great Bear Heart

We all read the note after she finished.

"You really think Norm Beeblemeyer will believe it?" I asked.

Shane Mitchell nodded. "He'll believe it, Parker," he assured. "Norm is just too nosy. He's always searching for some crazy story to dig up, and this will give him just what he's looking for. He's just *dying* to discover something like this."

Holly folded up the letter, put it in an envelope, and gave it to Dylan Bunker to run down to the post office.

"He'll get that note tomorrow," Shane said, "so we have some work to do. Tonight. Let's meet behind the library just after dark."

5

The Great Bear Heart library used to be an old train depot. The gray building sits right in front of Puckett Park, which, of course, is right on the shores of Puckett Lake. I was the first to get there, then Dylan Bunker, then Holly O'Mara, followed by Shane Mitchell and Tony Gritter. Lyle Haywood was the last to arrive.

We couldn't have picked a better night if we tried. There was no moon, and it was kind of chilly for a summer night, so there weren't any other people around. The air smelled of freshly-mowed lawns, and held a hint of wood smoke—someone, a few houses down from the park, was having a bonfire.

But what really helped us out was the fact that a thunderstorm had rolled through earlier in the evening, leaving the ground wet, soft and muddy. The tracks would be easy to make and easy to see in the soft earth. Conditions were *perfect*.

Tony Gritter was elected to be the one to wear the big feet, simply because he has longer legs than any of us. He could take much bigger strides—even bigger strides than Lyle Haywood—and could keep the footprints a few feet apart, making the creature seem big, and all the more menacing.

Which is about what you would expect from a giant, eight-foot hairy Bigfoot that was running amok in the forest around Great Bear Heart.

Holly and I stood watch near the library, and Dylan minded his post down by the water. Lyle Haywood was the lookout from the Great Bear Heart market, and he had one of our two-way radios. Shane had the other one, and he remained a short distance from Tony Gritter, who would be making the tracks in and around the park. Lyle was in a good place to see cars going by, or people approaching. If he thought that someone was coming, he would radio Shane, and the two could high-tail it into the woods before anyone spotted them.

Everything seemed to be going as planned. For a short time, all was quiet, and Holly and I remained as silent as we could, waiting, waiting . . . and waiting some more. We knew that, at that very moment, Tony Gritter was stomping through the dark park with the huge feet attached to his shoes. We couldn't see him, of course. All we could do was wait, and the anticipation was nerve-racking.

Twenty minutes later, I could hear excited whispering in the darkness as the two dark shapes of Shane Mitchell and Tony Gritter rushed toward us. Tony was carrying the enormous feet under his arm.

"Perfect!" Shane whispered loudly, his voice giddy with excitement.

"That's gonna be awesome!" Tony Gritter bragged.

"What do the footprints look like?" Holly asked.

"It's too dark to tell for sure," Shane answered, "but I think we pulled it off. I've got to believe that they look great! I can't wait till Norm Beeblemeyer gets that letter!"

Dylan Bunker wanted to come back in the morning to see what the big footprints looked like, but Shane disagreed. "Someone might see us," he said. "We can't be seen anywhere near those footprints, or else someone might suspect us later on. Let's just wait until Norm Beeblemeyer gets that letter. We have to be patient."

The next day, at exactly two forty-two in the afternoon, the phone rang at my house. It was Holly

O'Mara. Her voice was overflowing with excitement.

"Parker! You've got to come and see this!" she exclaimed.

"What?" I asked. "See what?"

"Down by the lake! Get down here! We're meeting at the hardware store in ten minutes!"

Things were about to go bonkers.

6

I expected to see Norm Beeblemeyer's car parked near the library, and maybe Norm trudging around the park with his camera.

What I *didn't* expect to see were the police cars and TV camera crews crammed in the small parking lot. There were dozens of people scurrying about, carrying cameras, clip-boards and notepads, looking all official-like. A yellow and black ribbon had been strung around the perimeter of the park, and uniformed police officers stood guard about every twenty feet. Police lights were flashing, groups of people were talking, and there were lots of arms pointing toward the park. It was utter madness.

Holly O'Mara was already in front of the hardware store, and I arrived at the same time as Dylan Bunker. Lyle and Tony rode up on their mountain bikes, and Shane Mitchell showed up a few minutes later, sprinting up to us, his face beat red from huffing and puffing. He had a smile on his face a mile wide.

"We did it!" he panted. "It worked! We really did it!"

"Just what did we do?" Holly asked nervously.

"We fooled Norm Beeblemeyer!" Shane replied, still gasping for air. "He bought into it hook, line, and sinker!"

"I think we fooled more people than just Norm Beeblemeyer," Lyle Haywood smirked, gazing at Puckett Park.

We all stared at the buzz of activity across the street. A TV crew was interviewing Norm Beeblemeyer, but we couldn't hear what he was saying. A policeman was talking to a few concerned residents that had gathered at the side of the road. A press conference was in session at one of the park picnic tables. A man wearing a black suit and a red tie was answering questions.

Tony Gritter and I were nominated to casually mosey on over to see what we could find out. We skipped across the highway and slipped innocently into the crowd of people.

The parking lot was so packed with people and vehicles that it was difficult to even walk through. Cars were parked only a few inches apart, but we managed to squeak by and make it down to the park.

I recognized Officer Hulburt, standing by a towering oak tree. He and my dad are friends, and had gone to school together. Officer Hulburt is pretty cool. He was the one who helped us out when Norm Beeblemeyer accused Tony Gritter of waxing the windows of the library. He saw us walking through the park, and we walked over to where he stood.

"Hey guys," he smiled warmly, waving as we approached.

"Hi, Officer Hulburt," I said, looking around at the confusion. "What's going on?"

Officer Hulburt shook his head, and a big smile came to his face. He looked like he was about to let us in on some big secret. "It's the craziest thing," he grinned, his cheeks glowing. "There are some strange footprints all around the park. Big ones. Like from some big creature or something. Far too big to be made by any human. Norm Beeblemeyer says he found them this morning."

"You don't say?!?!" I replied, trying to sound and look astonished. Inside, I was bursting with laughter. I know Tony was, too.

"Yeah, they're really something to see," Officer Hulbert whistled. "I can't let you back there right now, otherwise I'd let you guys go see for yourselves. They're bringing up some expert from the university to examine them later this afternoon."

My heart sank as I heard those words. An examiner from the university would surely discover that the giant footprints in the mud were phony, and then the jig would be up.

Rats.

"Well, what do they think it is?" Tony asked harmlessly.

"Beats me," Officer Hulburt shrugged, "but they say it looks like some big creature that walks upright on two legs. Like those Bigfoot creatures that are supposed to live out west. If you believe in those things, anyway."

We said good-bye to officer Hulburt and

walked back across the street to where Shane, Lyle, Holly, and Dylan were waiting. Their eyes were glued to all the excitement.

"It's working!" Tony Gritter snickered as we approached. He gave the 'thumbs up' signal, and his smile broadened. "They really think some kind of creature made those prints!"

"Of course they do," Lyle Haywood replied, matter-of-factly. "That's how we planned it."

"I just wish we could've been here to see Norm Beeblemeyer's face when he saw those tracks," Holly O'Mara confessed. "That sure would have been funny."

Across the street, the bustle of activity continued. Townspeople had gathered around the sidewalk in small clusters, talking about the mysterious creature that had made the huge footprints in the park. Ed Skinner, the town Mayor, was busy hustling from one group to the next, trying to pick up more and more bits of information. Lucy Marbles, better known as the town gossip, was doing the same, only she was making much more of an effort than Mayor Skinner. Lucy Marbles was a meddlesome, ornery woman with a penchant for sticking her nose where it didn't belong. She also had the benefit of a wild imagination, and I'm sure the Bigfoot story grew and grew with every person she spoke with.

But sadly, we knew that it would all be over later today. When the specialist from the university arrived, he would quickly determine that the footprints were fakes.

Oh well. It was kind of fun while it lasted. The tiny town of Great Bear Heart was at last seeing a bit of action, courtesy of the Adventure Club.

Of course, we didn't know it at the time, but the real fun was just about to begin.

7

The town of Great Bear Heart is named after an old Potowatami Indian Chief who lived here in the 1800s. Great Bear Heart, the town, is like a lot of other small towns in America: down-home folks who all pretty much know one another, people who look out for their neighbors. There are two churches, a post office and a township building, a hardware store, a bar and grill called *Rollers*, a market with gas pumps, a library, a thrift store, and a small restaurant called *The Kona*. A single, paved, two lane highway goes

213

through the middle of the town. There is also a network of blacktop roads that weave in and around a few small subdivisions. All in all, there are only several hundred people who live in Great Bear Heart.

But when gossip goes wild in Great Bear Heart—and often it does—it has a way of taking on a mind of its own.

By evening, Lucy Marbles had spread the rumor that dogs and cats had suddenly been missing around town, and she claimed the 'experts' were saying that Bigfoot could be responsible. At least this was the story that Lucy circulated. It was, of course, entirely untrue. She hadn't talked with any 'experts' any more than she had talked with a little man from Mars. But her pet story scared townsfolk into bringing in their dogs and cats from outside. Even Mayor Skinner, who has a goat, decided to bring the animal in for the night. I can't imagine a goat running around inside Mayor Skinner's house, and I know for a fact that Mrs. Skinner was pretty hot about the whole deal.

No one wanted to take any chances, though. After all, a dangerous, eight-foot, hairy creature was on the loose in Great Bear Heart.

Word got out that the expert from the

university had arrived, and that there would be a press conference in the parking lot of Puckett Park at eight o'clock. We all raced down there after dinner to hear the bad news broken.

The park was still filled with police cars and trucks, and two more TV stations had arrived. A large crowd had already started to gather, and people chattered among themselves in small groups. A microphone and speaker system had been set up, so that the growing swarm of residents would be able to hear what was being said.

"Don't you think that maybe we ought to keep a low profile?" I asked Shane. "After all, when they announce that this whole thing is a big fraud, Norm Beeblemeyer is going to suspect us right off the bat."

Shane shook his head. "I doubt it. And even if he does suspect us, he can't prove a thing."

At ten minutes past eight, an older, bespectacled man took the stage, holding a stack of papers in one hand, and a huge, white plaster cast of a footprint in the other. He had a scowl on his face and a stern look in his eyes. It was obvious that he was probably upset at the fact of being called all the way here, only to find that the whole thing had been a practical joke.

He leaned toward the microphone, and spoke.

"Ladies and Gentlemen," he began. His voice was rough, deep, and very serious. "Upon careful study of this rather extraordinary find, I am absolutely convinced that—"

The microphone suddenly went dead. His mouth continued to move, but we were too far away to hear what he was saying. Suddenly, a crewman from one of the television stations leapt forward, fiddled with some wires, and got the microphone working again.

"—as I was saying," the man began again. "This finding is truly one of monumental importance in the history of anthropology. These tracks, in my opinion, are indeed *genuine.*" He glanced at the plaster cast, and held it out for the crowd to see. "I believe that whatever made this footprint is still out here somewhere." He raised one arm and waved it slowly, as if denoting the forests around the small town.

A low gasp surged through the crowd of spectators, followed by a dramatic hush. A wave of fear washed over the spectators. The six of us just stared, mouths wide.

"I have seen many fakes in my life," the expert

216

continued, "and these, ladies and gentlemen, are definitely *not* fakes. I, for one, believe they were made by an unknown creature. A creature that many people have come to call 'Bigfoot'."

The crowd went wild. Newspaper people were busy scratching things down on notepads or typing furiously into laptop computers. Portable phones appeared out of nowhere, and the chattering reached a dull roar.

"Yes!" Tony Gritter softly hissed. He doubled his right hand into a fist and pounded the air. His smile was wide, and his eyes were on fire. *"It worked! It really worked!"*

The rest of us were too dumbstruck to say anything. We just watched the hordes of people rushing frantically about. Hands flew up in the air, questions were shouted. Still other people began devising plans to capture the great beast alive. More people ran home to make sure that their pets were safe indoors, thanks to the story made up by Lucy Marbles. The six of us stood silently beneath the awning of the hardware store, watching.

Finally, Holly O'Mara spoke up. "Now what?" she asked, posing the question to club president Shane Mitchell.

It was a good question. I guess we all just figured that Norm Beeblemeyer would maybe take some photos of the footprints and put them in the paper, and later on we could somehow call his bluff, and everybody in town would realize that Norm had been had. None of us expected that the whole thing would get blown out of proportion like this. I think that some of us were even a bit worried. I know I was.

But not Shane Mitchell. He had his infamous smirk that told us that he'd thought up another plan.

And I must admit, this one was bound to be one of his better ones.

8

Shane called for an early meeting the very next morning, and we all gathered at the clubhouse at eight, sharp. We were all on time except for Dylan Bunker, who arrived his typical fifteen minutes late.

"Okay, what's up?" Lyle Haywood asked Shane. Shane wouldn't tell us last night what he'd planned, but wanted to wait until this morning. We were all anxious to find out what he had up his sleeve.

"How much money is the club in the hole for?" Shane asked Holly. Holly O'Mara recited the number from memory, which is one of the reasons why she makes such a good club treasurer. She looked up at the ceiling, as if drawing the numbers from the air.

"Including all of the money that the club owes each of us, and the ten dollars that Lyle Haywood borrowed from his dad, the club owes forty seven dollars and twenty eight cents."

"Suppose," Shane began, "we can pay all of that back today, and even make enough to have a surplus in our coffee can?" Our coffee can was where we kept the club money. It was stashed under a log in the woods not far from the clubhouse.

We all stared at Shane. We couldn't figure out where he was going with this one.

"Okay, here's the situation," he continued. He leaned forward on the milk crate and folded his hands. His eyes drifted to each one of us as he spoke. "There's going to be lots of people down at the park today, right?" We all nodded our heads. There was sure to be a ton of people pouring into Great Bear Heart. "Scads of people are going to be looking for that creature," Shane continued, his eyes burning with excitement. "There's only one restaurant in town, and one market. The restaurant is too small to feed all those people, and the market will be jammed all day long."

Lyle Haywood began to smile. The rest of us still didn't figure what he was getting at just yet.

"What I'm saying," Shane Mitchell continued, the smile on his face growing, "is that the Adventure Club Roadside Diner is now open for business."

9

By nine-thirty there was already a good crowd of people milling about Puckett Park. By ten, the single highway through town was nearly at a standstill. Cars, filled with gawkers and sightseers, crept along like snails, all hoping to get a glimpse at the mysterious beast.

And by ten-thirty, the Adventure Club Roadside Diner had officially opened.

We had three card tables lined up. Holly and I took orders for cold beverages, while Tony Gritter grilled hot dogs and hamburgers on a small gas grill set up behind us. The grill belonged to Shane Mitchell's mom and dad, and he'd managed to somehow sneak it from their deck and wheel it down the hill to the park without his parents knowing about it.

Lyle Haywood made a big wood sign to advertise, and leaned it up against a nearby tree. He'd come up with some clever names, too. We had 'Bigfoot Burgers' and 'Carnivore Corn Dogs.' The hamburgers and corn dogs came from Holly O'Mara's house, but we ran out pretty fast. Which was okay, because we'd already made enough money to run across to the market and buy more hamburger ourselves. George Bloomer, the owner of the market, was glad to see our operation in full swing. He said his small store couldn't handle all of the business anyway, so we weren't taking any sales away from him by putting up a stand across from his store. In fact, he said that he'd sold more hamburger meat to us in one morning than he usually sells all week, so he was glad for our business.

Our beverages were hot sellers as well. Lyle called the Lemonade 'Monster Juice'. He'd originally called our iced-tea 'Bigfoot Blood' but with a name like that, we didn't sell much, as you can imagine why. When he changed the name to 'Sasquatch Quencher', we sold oodles of the stuff. Marketing, as they say, is *everything*.

Our customers were anyone and everyone. Thirsty townspeople gulped down the lemonade by the gallon. Television crews would send one of their workers over to order for their colleagues, and some of them ordered eight or ten burgers at a time. We were so busy that Shane Mitchell took over grilling duties for a while so Lyle Haywood could go find another grill. He wound up sneaking one from his own house, just like Shane Mitchell had done.

"Carnivore Corn Dogs!" Dylan Bunker hawked. "Get your Carnivore Corn Dogs, just one dollar!"

"Monster Juice, just seventy-five cents!" Holly O'Mara chirped.

A line began to form at all three tables, and we couldn't serve our customers fast enough. The money just kept rolling in.

In short, the Adventure Club Roadside Diner was a smash success. By noon, the club had made enough money to pay each of us back. By three o'clock, we'd cleared nearly seventy-five dollars, and that was *after* expenses. George Bloomer finally let us charge the food items we needed, and we agreed to pay our bill at the end of the day.

At seven o'clock that evening we called it quits for the day, paid George Bloomer what we owed his store, and met back at the clubhouse. Holly counted up the money and divided up what was owed to each of us. Dylan Bunker was overjoyed. After everyone was paid back, we'd cleared one hundred thirty-three dollars and six cents. Not only had we been able to pay everyone back, but we had some money in our coffee can to boot. I went to bed that night with dollar signs in my eyes. We'd made a ton of money — and the next day would be even better.

Or so we thought.

10

We'd planned to get the Adventure Club Roadside Diner started at ten o'clock the next morning — *but someone else beat us to it!*

When I saw the stand already set up in front of the park, I'd figured that Shane and Lyle arrived early to get things set up. But when I got closer, I realized that they weren't our tables at all.

Someone had swiped our spot!

Not only that, but they'd put up their own sign . . . in the exact same spot we'd had ours the day before! They called their stand the 'Creature Cafe'. They were selling hot dogs and hamburgers, and lemonade and iced-tea, just like we had done yesterday!

Instantly, I knew who it was.

The Martin brothers. All three of them, to be exact. Terry, Gary, and Larry. We should have expected it. If there's anyone who would do such a thing, it would be them. They've given all of us trouble for a long time, and we have a sneaking suspicion that they were the ones who waxed the windows at the library. In fact, all three of them were, at one time, Boy Scouts. All three were kicked out within a year for disobedience. They missed meetings, didn't follow directions, and broke just about every rule the Scouts had. None of them had even bothered to try and earn any merit badges, and only Gary progressed passed the rank of Tenderfoot. All three Martin brothers were jerks, plain and simple.

I kept my distance and hung out at the hardware store, watching the roadside stand. Holly O'Mara finally showed up, and she, too, was dumbfounded when she saw the Martin's stand across the street.

"What . . . what in the world is going on?!?!?"

she stammered.

I couldn't answer her. I just shook my head.

After a few more minutes, the rest of the club arrived. Shane, Tony, Lyle, Dylan, Holly, and I stood under the awning of the hardware store, watching the Martin brothers. Not one of us said a thing.

The situation looked grim. We couldn't put up another stand right next to the Martin's. I mean, I guess we could, but we'd certainly make a lot less money than we did the day before.

It wasn't fair. The Martin brothers had stolen our idea.

And to make matters worse, every once in a while, Terry, who was the oldest of the brothers, would look over at all of us and give us a sarcastic smile . . . usually right after he'd sold another hamburger or hot dog.

Shane called an emergency meeting at the clubhouse in an hour, exactly. He said that he'd need some time to set up a few things. What those 'things' were, he wouldn't say. He said that we'd know soon enough.

In exactly one hour, we were all at the clubhouse, except for Dylan, who was fifteen minutes late, as usual.

Shane called the meeting to order without Dylan, and he didn't waste any time in issuing directives.

"Tony," he ordered, "you and Lyle go set up the roadside stand across from *Lazy Shores Resort.*" *Lazy Shores Resort* was a small resort on the shores of Puckett Lake, about a quarter of a mile south of the park. There were eight separate cabins, all placed alongside one another. It was pretty busy all summer long, as it was the only place of its kind in Great Bear Heart. The cabins were rented to vacationing tourists.

"But that's a long ways away from anyone!" Holly pleaded. "The people are down at the park!"

Just then, Dylan popped his head through the trap door.

"Sorry I'm late, guys," he apologized, scrambling through the floor and taking his usual seat against the wall.

"Dylan," Shane Mitchell commanded, as though Dylan had been there all along, "you'll help me load up my Dad's golf cart down at the market."

A lot of people have golf carts in Great Bear Heart. Since the town is so small, lots of folks use golf carts, instead of cars, to run their errands.

Shane looked at Holly O'Mara. "Holly, you go

with Lyle and Tony and get the Monster Juice and Sasquatch Quencher ready. Those coolers will be heavy, and they'll need all the help they can get." He looked at me. "Parker, I need you to make an important phone call."

"But Shane," Tony interjected, "there's hardly anyone down at *Lazy Shores Resort*. Like Holly said — they're all down at the park!"

Shane flashed a confident smile, and we all hoped he knew what he was doing. "Not for long, they won't be," was all he said. "Not for long."

11

Shane had given me careful instructions. I waited at my house until he called, then I hung up, picked the phone back up again—and dialed the number to the local radio station.

I told them that my name was Arnie Zarshaken, and that I had just spotted a giant, ape-like creature in the woods—right across from *Lazy Shores Resort*. I hung up, hopped on my bike, and high-tailed it to meet Shane Mitchell downtown.

Dylan and Shane were at the hardware store,

perched on the seats of their mountain bikes, watching the huge crowd in the park. They had just returned from our stand that Holly, Tony, and Lyle were setting up across from *Lazy Shores Resort*.

The Martin brothers were doing a great business. There were two lines of people waiting to get served. I was still hopping mad about how they had stolen our idea. They had stolen our idea—*and* our customers.

Things were about to change.

Suddenly, people began running to their cars! Just like we'd hoped, the radio station had contacted their crew at Puckett Park, telling them that the creature had been spotted a quarter of a mile away . . . near the *Lazy Shores Resort!*

Car engines roared, and vehicles spun out of the parking lot. People that were waiting in line at the food stand suddenly bolted in every direction. There was so much confusion that one of the cars bumped into one of the tables where the Martin brothers were selling food, and fifty gallons of lemonade tipped over in one giant gush, splattering all over the gravel shoulder. Larry tried to save the huge cooler before it went over, but only succeeded in knocking over two full tins of hamburgers that had yet to be cooked. The meat tumbled into the gravel and dirt. A little black dog that was scampering through the park caught wind of the upended burgers, and began hungrily gobbling them up. Gary Martin looked comical chasing the little dog around the park, trying to keep him from eating the meat.

It was chaotic. TV crews hurriedly packed up their gear and sped off. Police cars, sirens blaring, roared away from the scene.

Satisfied, Shane looked at his watch.

"Right on time!" he exclaimed urgently. "Let's go!"

Loose dirt spun beneath our bicycle tires. We were off, pedaling like mad down the shoulder of the road.

In seconds, we were in front of *Lazy Shores Resort*, where a large crowd was already growing. Most of the people that had been down at the park were now swarming the area around the *Lazy Shores Resort*. Everyone was on the lookout for Bigfoot.

Shane's plan had been simple, and it worked like a charm. In the hour before the meeting that he needed to 'set things up' he had sneaked into the woods adjacent to the *Lazy Shores Resort*. He plodded around with the big feet strapped to his shoes, making big imprints in the ground near the lake and along a small creek. I, of course, didn't see them, but Shane said that the footprints looked awesome—and, after my phone call to the radio station, it didn't take long for someone to find them.

"Over here!" we heard an unseen voice shout. Frantic scrambling ensued as people began dashing through the woods. Branches snapped as a hoard of people thundered through the woods. A police megaphone barked orders for people to stay back, that the creature could be dangerous. The only thing that they found, obviously, were tracks from the beast, but there were a few nervous moments as people looked behind thick brush piles to see if the creature had gone into hiding. One of the police officers, fearful that the creature could be near, drew his gun as a precaution.

It took about a half an hour for the initial excitement to wear off, and for things to get busy at our roadside stand. At first, people were too interested in seeing the large tracks in the mud than they were eating food, so business was slow. But as news leaked out, more and more people showed up, clogging the highway and slowing traffic to a standstill. Soon, hundreds of people were combing

the area around *Lazy Shores Resort*.
And our business skyrocketed.

12

Later that night at our meeting, we counted up the money. One hundred seventy-seven dollars and forty-eight cents! That gave us a grand total of three hundred ten dollars and fifty-four cents for both days! I had never seen so much money.

The local paper, the *Great Bear Heart Times*, printed their weekly edition early because of the sensation. Lyle Haywood brought a copy to the meeting. A picture of the beast's footprint was on the front page, along with a picture of Norm

Beeblemeyer — and boy, was Norm full of himself. He stated in his story that he'd been investigating the strange creature for weeks, and that he had actually spotted the creature in the hills just beyond Great Bear Heart.

"That's a flat-out lie!" Tony Gritter flared angrily. "He's making it all up!"

Norm Beeblemeyer had gone on to write that *he* had been the one to discover the huge prints in the park, after his 'weeks upon weeks of scouring the forest'. He made no mention of the letter he had received — the letter *we* had made up and sent him!

"He's hogging all of the attention himself," I fumed. "That's not fair!"

"Relax," Shane Mitchell said, trying to cool things off. "That's just what we want, isn't it? Let him have his fifteen minutes of fame. This whole thing will backfire on him somehow. You watch."

Shane was wrong . . . because things weren't quite about to backfire for Norm Beeblemeyer.

Oh, they were about to backfire, all right — on us.

The next day, a coincidental chain of events occurred that can only be described as 'bizarre'. They began with a frantic phone call from Shane Mitchell to

Tony Gritter. It was just past eight in the morning.

"Tony! The feet! They're gone!!" His voice was flooded with panic.

"What are you talking about?!?!" Tony asked groggily. The phone call had awoken him from a sound sleep.

"I went to get them out of the garage this morning, but they're gone!" Shane explained. "The only thing there is an empty bag!"

This sounded the alarm, and we held yet another emergency meeting at the clubhouse. We were all talking and trying to figure out what had happened to the feet. Dylan Bunker was his usual fifteen minutes late, but this time we heard him coming from across the field and up the rope ladder. He was running at full bore—something Dylan Bunker never did. Dylan is usually so slow that if he moved any faster, he'd be going backwards.

He burst through the floor all out of breath, huffing and puffing like a sick dragon.

"What's up with you?" Lyle Haywood asked as Dylan collapsed in a heap on the clubhouse floor.

"Tracks," he gasped in between giant gulps of air. His cheeks were red and puffy from running so hard. "There are tracks—Bigfoot tracks—*all over town!"*

"What?!?!" Shane exclaimed. "Did you see them??!"

Dylan nodded his head. "Yep! And man, they're *everywhere!*"

This was a disaster. Bigfoot tracks around town meant two things: first, someone had obviously stolen our wooden Bigfoot feet, but most importantly, someone knew that we were behind the whole thing! We'd been found out!

"Okay, okay, let's keep a clear head about his," Tony Gritter reasoned. "So, someone's got our big feet. All we have to do is find out who."

"I'll bet it's the Martin brothers," Holly O'Mara said coldly. Her cheeks were flushed in anger, and she clenched her teeth. "I'll bet they're behind this."

"That doesn't make sense, though," Shane replied. "They had no idea what we were up to. Even if they did, those feet were hidden away in a burlap bag. They would have never found them."

By the time the six of us high-tailed it to town, the mood was frantic. Just like Dylan said, there were Bigfoot tracks everywhere. People scrambled all over the village, snapping pictures, pointing, trying to find out where the huge creature had been and where he might be headed.

Suddenly, Shane Mitchell's face turned white. His mouth opened, and his eyes popped right out of his head.

"The Martin brothers weren't behind this!" he exclaimed, slapping a palm to his forehead. "I'll bet you a buffalo nickel that it was my kid brother! He's a nosy little bugger! I'll bet he was playing in the garage and found the feet! Oh Man! Why didn't I think of that in the first place?!?!"

We were in a jam. If Shane's little brother was indeed the culprit, it meant that, sooner or later, he would be heading home . . . with Bigfoot tracks winding all the way up to Shane's house!

"Come on!" Lyle Haywood shouted. "We've got to make it back to Shane's house before anyone else does!"

We were off. To make things a bit less conspicuous, we all left in different directions, circling the neighborhood, in case Shane's little brother wasn't headed for home. Shane would head straight back to his house, while the rest of us split up and took different routes.

True to Shane's suspicions, we found tracks heading up to his house. His little brother must have taken the feet early in the morning. While we had been holding our emergency meeting, the little thief was running around town creating havoc. It was amazing that he hadn't been spotted by someone already.

But we knew it was only a matter of time. There were other people hot on the trail as well. They were following the footprints . . . and it wasn't going to take them long to find out where the tracks were headed.

13

I took off on my bike and headed around to the back of Shane's house, so I would come in from a totally different direction than everyone else. There are a lot of trails that wind through the woods around neighborhood, and we all know them like the backs of our hands. I hoped I could make it without being seen and arousing any suspicion.

Coming up behind Shane's house, I stashed my bike in the brush and scouted out the area. There was no sign of anyone yet . . . *except Ryan, Shane's little brother!*

Oh no!

He was coming up the driveway, with the enormous feet strapped to his shoes! His steps were clumsy and difficult. Ryan is seven years old . . . the wooden feet were far too big for him to be walking with, but he was managing, somehow.

And he looked like he was having the time of his life! Every couple of steps he would stop, turn around, look at the footprints he had just made, and giggle.

Step, step, stop, giggle. Step, step, stop, giggle. Ryan was having a blast.

There was no time to lose.

"Ryan!" I shouted, sprinting across the yard. I ran as fast as my legs would carry me. Surprised, Ryan stopped where he was, staring at me. I ran up to him.

"Ryan, I need you to do a favor for me. Can you go down to the market and get me a candy bar?" I stuffed my hand into my pocket and pulled out a dollar. "If you do, you can buy one for yourself. Free. But I need you to hurry, so you'll have to leave those big feet here."

I didn't have to ask him twice. He stared at the

dollar in my hand, then reached down and unsnapped the huge feet from his shoes. In a flash, he was off. The whole exchange took ten seconds.

I had to act fast. I was certain that there were people following the tracks Ryan had made. They would be here any second.

But I had a plan.

Without wasting another moment, I buckled the wooden feet to my shoes and took off across the yard in a near run. It was pretty hard going with those huge feet strapped to my sneakers, but I managed. I was careful to pick every soft spot in the ground that I could. I wanted to make sure that whoever was following the tracks would be able to find them easily.

I skirted the house and snuck off into the woods—and not a moment too soon. I heard a car coming, and I turned to see a police cruiser moving slowly along the driveway, along with a few people walking slowly next to it! They were all staring at the ground, following the tracks. Flashbulbs were popping, and people were looking anxiously around. They knew they were getting close to Bigfoot.

There's a small stream in the woods not too far from Shane's house, and I headed for it. I sure hoped my idea would work! If I could pull it off, we could wrap up this whole thing without anyone being the wiser. Granted, it was a pretty daring plan, but at the time it seemed like my only option. In fact, the only other option at the time was to get caught — in the act.

No way, I thought, as I lumbered through the forest with the big feet strapped to my shoes. Branches smacked my head, and twice I almost fell.

At the creek, I turned and followed it downstream, making sure my tracks were visible in the black muck. I wanted to be certain that the people following me wouldn't lose my trail.

The creek winds south of town, passes just beyond the *Lazy Shores Resort,* goes under the highway, and then flows into Puckett Lake. My plan was to follow the creek down to the lake and weave my way back to the park, where the tracks would get lost among all of the other tracks.

If I wasn't spotted, anyway.

I could hear branches crunching and breaking behind me, and I knew that the Bigfoot hunters weren't far off. I was glad that they hadn't brought any dogs along! I'd be a goner, for sure.

But as I sloshed along through the mud next to the creek, I also began to realize that there was no way I was going to make it back to the park. My pursuers were too close. I was going to be caught red-handed!

I trudged on. I wound around and behind *Lazy Shores Resort,* keeping an eye out for anyone that might spot me. I did see a few people, but they seemed distracted by other things that were going on across the street.

I had to think fast. I was pretty much out in the open, and I could be spotted real easy. It's hard to miss a thirteen year-old with small canoes on his feet.

Think. *Think.*

I was standing near the edge of the forest, frantically wondering what to do, listening to the breaking branches and twigs in the forest behind me. The pursuers were coming closer, and in a few minutes they would be coming through the brush.

Then, I spotted Norm Beeblemeyer's parked car.

14

In five minutes, the noisy group of searchers emerged from the forest. They were tense and their heads turned as they stepped out into the open, for they knew that they were closing in on the dangerous Bigfoot creature.

I was standing at our roadside stand, getting things ready for the day, sipping on a glass of Monster Juice. Moments after the Bigfoot search party had emerged from the forest, Holly O'Mara came speeding up on her bike, followed by Lyle Haywood.

Shane Mitchell wasn't far behind, followed by Tony Gritter and Dylan Bunker. I wore a grin from ear to ear, and I acted like I hadn't a care in the world.

"Parker! What's going on?!?" Holly asked, leaning her bike against a tree and running up to me.

I just smiled. Shane, Tony, Dylan and Lyle all rushed up to the stand.

"Don't look so nervous, guys," I coaxed. "Relax. Just pretend that nothing's going on."

The group of searchers hastily crossed the highway and picked up the huge tracks once again, following them through the dirt, around a mostly-dried mud puddle—and right up to the passenger door of Norm Beeblemeyer's car.

"Parker, you didn't!" Shane exclaimed in disbelief. His eyes never left the growing group of people next to Norm Beeblemeyer's car.

"I did," I smirked.

The group around Norm's car began to get noisy and loud, and we could tell they were thoroughly disgusted. Someone opened up the car door and pulled out two very large wooden feet—and held them up for the gathering crowd to see.

15

Norm Beeblemeyer had a lot of explaining to do. Of course, everyone knew that he hadn't been the one who had led the group on the goose chase, since he was with the party of searchers that had followed the tracks through the woods and along the stream and back to his car. But everyone figured that somehow, Norm was in on the whole scheme, even though they couldn't prove it.

The next week's paper printed an apology and a retraction from Norm, saying that he'd been 'caught up in all the excitement' and that he had been 'carried away'. He adamantly insisted that he didn't have anything to do with the Bigfoot tracks, but not many people believed him. He'd been caught with the wooden feet in his car. Norm Beeblemeyer had egg all over his face, and there were at least six people in the town of Great Bear Heart that thought he got exactly what was coming to him.

At our next meeting, we spent the first half hour talking about the Bigfoot adventure. Dylan had a copy of the paper, and we took turns reading it out loud, giggling to ourselves.

"Serves him right!" Tony Gritter exclaimed, after reading Norm's apology.

We all laughed about it for a while, and thought that the whole Bigfoot episode would be the most fun we'd have all summer.

That is, of course, until the day Lyle Haywood found the old, beat-up submarine in Alfred Franklin's junkyard.

That's when things got *really* crazy . . . .

GHOST IN THE GRAVEYARD

is the first compilation of short stories from Michigan author Johnathan Rand! Stories include 'Bigfoot Runs Amok', 'The Hidden Door', 'Ghost in the Graveyard', and MORE!

"These stories are TOO COOL!" - Justin G., age 11, Chicago, IL

"GREAT STORIES! If you like the 'Chillers' series, you'll love 'GHOST IN THE GRAVEYARD'! - Amanda K., age 9, Livonia, MI

'GHOST IN THE GRAVEYARD' is awesome! I can't wait for more books like this one!" - Tyler S., age 13, Denver, CO.

"All of my students LOVE 'GHOST IN THE GRAVEYARD'!"
- Bryan Randle, teacher, Gladwin, MI

Find out more at
www.ghostinthegraveyard.net

257

SINISTER SPIDERS OF SAGINAW WORD SEARCH!

```
R O G T G M U K D E R R A J H G R W Z C
G Y N M P L U Z N P F D F X P B E A O I
E V B A L U T N A R A T A K U B J N M Y
M W K P Q Q M A R E G V K R U F N I J V
G E S Q M H Z E N T B T G I D E C G L Y
Z X I R R V L N A S D T G S R H V A D E
R M Z Y E B I S H I G N I T A L C S Y T
I V Q R M L V N T N Z A S E I D E Q D B
Z R S M E A L E A I T L L N N S W U A M
H B P H R C B I N S B P R S A R O Y J G
B G K O S K E P H J Z R A N G E L A Z S
U T V G O W G A O C O E V S E Y O S E S
I E H L N I D S J R N T M R D N H A Z E
I U C J V D C O E D A A J E I G B K A F
V I T M R O I N K R Z W G D T W W U H J
S P B Q W W C H R N O F E I C J V G A S
W U I Z O Z L C G T R G Y P H J S O E M
Y Q Q B O T S A J L R P O S Y C B C L J
R E E H X A F R W U Q R H T Y B I D F G
O H W P B R N A M E V Q B R C D H M D Y
Z C W A B H R P S O K Q Q F I O N I L P
L P Q F R G Y I U P N I B C Z O Q W Y S
O A J I Z Q E C A W F A A L J C H V G A
B W H T J A Q H O J P L G W O S Z D U X
```

*Octogores *Mr. Emerson *Conner *Leah *Angela
*Jarred *Spiders *Arachno-Sapiens *Saginaw
*Grumpy   *Michigan Chillers   *Water Plant
*Sinister *Drainage Ditch *Acid Ice   *Web
*Tarantula   *Black Widow *Johnathan Rand

WORD SCRAMBLE!
Unscramble the letters to form a word!

WGNAAIS _ _ _ _ _ _ _

DAIC EIC _ _ _ _ _ _ _

IRDSSPE _ _ _ _ _ _ _

EJDRAR _ _ _ _ _ _

GAIHNMIC ESHLCIRL _ _ _ _ _ _ _ _ _ _ _ _ _ _ _

RCENON _ _ _ _ _ _

RMPGYU _ _ _ _ _ _

AEHL _ _ _ _

RM RSEOMNE _ _ _ _ _ _ _ _ _

ITRNISSE _ _ _ _ _ _ _ _

NNAJOHAHT RDNA _ _ _ _ _ _ _ _ _ _ _ _ _

GRTOCOEO _ _ _ _ _ _ _ _

RAUNAATTL _ _ _ _ _ _ _ _

LKBCA OWDIW _ _ _ _ _ _ _ _ _ _

Join Johnathan Rand as he travels! Check out *www.michiganchillers.com* for Mr. Rand's on-line journal, featuring pictures and stories during his journeys! It's like traveling with him yourself! You'll get the inside scoop on when and where he'll be, and what projects he's working on right now! *Visit www.michiganchillers.com!*

About the cover art: This unique cover was designed and created by Michigan artists Darrin Brege and Mark Thompson.

Darrin Brege works as an animator by day, and is now applying his talents on the internet, creating various web sites and flash animations. He attended animation school in southern California in the early nineties, and over the years has created original characters and animations for Warner Bros (Space Jam), for Hasbro (Tonka Joe Multimedia line), Universal Pictures (Bullwinkle and Fractured Fairy Tales CD Roms), and Disney. Besides art, he and his wife Karen are improv performers featured weekly at Mark Ridley's Comedy Castle over the last six years. Improvisational comedy has provided the groundwork for a successful voice over career as well. Darrin has dozens of characters and impersonations in his portfolio and, most recently, provided Columbia Tri-Star pictures with a Nathan Lane 'sound alike' for Stuart Little. Speaking of little, Darrin and Karen also have a little son named Mick.

Mark Thompson, also known as THE ICEMAN, has been in the illustration field for over 20 years, working for everyone from the Detroit Tigers, Ameritech, as well as auto companies and toy companies such as Hasbro and Mattel. Mark's main interests are in science fiction and fantasy art. He works from his studio in a log home in the woods of Hamburg, Michigan. Mark is married with 2 children, and he is also a big-time horror fan and comic collector!

About the author

Much has changed for Johnathan Rand and his wife since the introduction of the 'Michigan Chillers' series. The books have become one of the best-selling series in the Midwest, with over 150,000 copies in print. When they are not traveling to schools and book signings, Mr. Rand and his wife live in a small town in northern lower Michigan. He still writes all of his books in the wee hours of the morning, and still submits all manuscripts by mail. And yes, Johnathan Rand is still afraid of the dark . . . which may explain why he stays up all night and sleeps during the day.

For information regarding author appearances,
school visits, or book signings, write to:

AudioCraft Publishing, Inc.
PO Box 281
Topinabee Island, MI 49791

or call
(231) 238-4424